1

ISBN: 978-0-578-65217-7
LCCN: 2020904478

Any references to historical events, real people, or real places are used fictitiously. Names, characters, and places are products of the author's imagination.

Printed by KDP, in the United States of America.

First printing edition 2020.

C.J. Sampera
180 Smoketree Ave
Oak Park, CA 91377

Unsettling Legends

By C.J. Sampera

Dedicated to my wife and my little ghouls who inspire me every day, and to all the creators who came before me that lit a spark in this deep dark maze & showed me the way.

What Darkness we Keep

What crawls and creeps

What lies In the Deep

Foreword

Reader beware: These legends are riddled with horror and terror, though as the title suggests, many of these stories are more unsettling than they are scary. Each one is told from a different perspective as they were once told to me. From the malicious mistreatment of a mythical creature to the insidious side effects of a futuristic supplement, these tales are wrought with discomfort and dread, they are designed to make you feel squeamish. There are no happy endings here. So be warned and be brave dear reader, and prepare yourself for 16 extremely,
Unsettling
Legends

WHAT DARKNESS WE KEEP

From buried bones in ancient tombs, to shadows cast
from passing moons
In story and song we speak of scars so we remember all our
wounds
We keep these creeping fears, inside the folklore we've
amassed
What dark and dreary things do you hold on to from the
past?

OX & CROW

BURDEN:

Quite some time ago… when the world was still fresh and new, there lived a massive black ox whose name was Burden. Horns of iron and ash, skin tougher than railroad tracks, his coarse wooly fur a shade of black so dark that he looked like a hole in the Earth. Burden was born fully grown with a massive saddle bag strapped across his hulking back. His sole purpose was to carry the weight of our worries and troubles and fears, carry them right to the edge of the world and do away with them. The load was always incredibly heavy but Burden was the strongest Ox in this galaxy and the next, and Burden did his duty without so much as a word or a grumbling. And so, the weight of our worries would drift away and the world was a much happier place because of it.

Burden would travel from village to village with his pack and the villagers would come throw every bad bone they could pick inside. Once his bag was full, he would start his journey to the ends of the world. Through fire, through brimstone, through the deepest darkest, over towering mountains, and into the abyss. Burden would carry his bag of bones to the very last patch of dirt and ashen rock, right to the edge of the globe. He would empty them out and every bone and bad dream the people had bestowed upon him would fall into the great wide nothing and fade into patches of the night sky.

He never asked why, he never complained. Burden knew it was his purpose and he kept his head low as if he was perpetually bowing to Mother Earth.

In the beginning, the people of Earth were grateful. They would bring him baskets of lush greens to eat and fresh water to drink and thank him for his cumbersome sacrifice. However, as time went on the people became so accustomed to Burden's service that it was no longer celebrated and lauded, it was expected and greatly unappreciated. They did not bring him food or water, they no longer gave thanks, they did not await his arrival with bated breath. Now they were impatient and listless. They unloaded their bones into his bag with disdain, as if it were a chore. Some even yelled at him to "Hurry up!"

Still, Burden never batted an eye. He kept his head low and carried out his commitment without a second thought as he really didn't have many thoughts at all. He did what he was made to do and nothing more. Nothing less. The way he always had, the way he always would. Or rather, he would have, if it were not for one particularly mettlesome crow.

CHAOS:

Chaos the crow lived high in the trees and ruled over the sky. Chaos was rather large for a bird, sleek and black... so much so that it almost looked as if he was always moving, even when sitting completely still. Chaos has existed since Burden began to walk the Earth, though they are both quite the opposite. Chaos is loud and obnoxious, unpredictable and seemingly everywhere at once (which allowed him to stick his beak in all the places that it did not belong.)

Chaos always watched Burden carefully, he was jealous of his uniformity and consistency. He didn't understand his mission or why he was obligated to help the humans that he served, the humans Chaos so detested. So, every year, he would try and thwart Burden's journey. He would come up with new and inventive ways to try and stop the ox but Burden never gave way, he carried right along moving the weight of the world on his shoulders. Year after year he tried, and every year Chaos failed. Not to be undone, Chaos had a spirit just as indomitable as the beast and after a while he began to admire and gain a great deal of respect for his immovable adversary.

But when Chaos saw how those he served had begun to treat Burden, he became enraged. He could not begin to fathom how or why these mortals could take such a magnificent deity for granted. Chaos landed in the town square and started squawking madly at the villagers, "This magnificent ox is a creature of the Gods as am I and we shall

11

be exalted as such! You fools should be groveling at his feet! Yet you dare to slight him? You dare gaze upon this gift from the heavens begrudgingly? For shame!" Chaos flapped his wings and thunderous black clouds unfurled out from under them and into the sky. Thunder rumbled as he took in heaving breaths, eyes darting from face to face of the crowd that had started to gather. And then, the people simply dispersed. They shrugged their shoulders, they rolled their eyes, not a soul could be bothered to care.

Chaos spent days and nights trying to think of a plan to make the humans see the error in their ways and pay Burden the respect he was due. The villagers knew Chaos was a thief and a trickster, he couldn't talk to them himself. He knew there was no talking to the ox, let alone stopping him, it would be like preaching caution to a speeding boulder rolling down a mountain. Fruitless. Hopeless.

"What to do, what to do!" He cawed frantically as he hopped back and forth on his perch and plucked at his own feathers, "I haven't a clue, what one could possibly do... I'm shedding, I'm molting, I'm out of my head... I haven't a clue, I'm losing the... thread!"

Chaos stood absolutely still for possibly the first time in his entire existence. His black eyes gleamed with cunning and pride.

"That's it. One little thread. It's all that I need."

And so, with his ever watchful and incredibly accurate eye, Chaos waited and watched until he finally spotted what he wanted. One tiny strand of thread dangling from the bottom of Burden's bag. Chaos smirked to himself and waited some more. He waited until every last bone had been thrown apathetically into Burdens bag, he waited until Burden was well out of town and deep into the forest. There, Chaos plopped down only about a foot behind the meandering missionary and hopped along keeping perfect pace. Every couple of feet, he would pull at the strand with his beak. Little by little... a small tear began to unravel at the bottom of the bag. More and more until the tear became a hole. Chaos poked at the hole with his beak, carefully so as not to disturb the beast but with just the right amount of force to make the hole just big enough for the little nitpicky bones of the villagers to tumble out, one by one. And as each bone fell Chaos picked up each and every one and flew them back to the village, carefully making little nests of bones and dread, right outside the homes of each of their respective owners.

As each nest appeared, all the fear and worry and terror came rushing back to the world. It was a very new and very strange, terrible feeling for the people. Chaos was brimming with glee when he saw the woe on their faces, a look he thought to himself that was beyond well deserved. He saw the expression on every single one and drank it in like a fine wine. What Chaos did not see however, was what happened to his ill-fated adversary.

As each bone had dropped from Burden's bounty, his load became lighter and lighter. Burden was not used to having such little weight to carry at this part in his journey and so he thought surely, he still had a way to go, and yet he was three steps from the end of the Earth...

in four steps,

Burden was gone.

Burden fell to the stars, returned to the sky, and was dispersed in tiny morsels back to the humans who in turn digested their pain and now carried the weight of their own personal burden... and Chaos reigned forever more.

13

Tatamukage (Folding Shadows)

My father always told me not to play with fire because if you do, you'll wet the bed. My father also told me that if you feel a cold sensation in your belly, it means you'll soon have diarrhea. My father fed me tons of old crazy superstitions over the years and for a long time, I believed every one of them.

I used to watch the sidewalk on my way to school in the morning and did my absolute best to step over every single crack that I crossed. Over time though, believing in superstitions is just stressful and downright silly. One of the silliest things my dad ever told me, and he really wouldn't let this one go, was to never-under any circumstances-never ever walk your dog or let your animals out at night. For if you did, they would surely meet the Tatamukage.

According to my father the Tatamukage were giant monsters who lurked in the darkness outside, hiding behind the trees, and if they saw or even smelled an animal walking across their path... They would unfold from out of the shadows. (Yes, he said their bodies would unfold like giant shadowy pieces of origami, *crazy* right?) He said they were tall and lanky and completely made of shadows and darkness, the only thing you could see were two tiny white glowing eyes in their head. He said they would snap and pop and let out a low, rumbling growl as they unfolded out of the trees. Then they stretched their long, crooked arms out to grab any animals they could find... and swallow them whole.

Dad also said that once they take your dog or your cat, they'll follow you home. He says that they'll just wait around the trees outside of your house, folding in and out of the shadows, waiting for you to bring them another snack.

I told my dad that his superstitions were old, and crazy, and didn't really translate well to this day and age in America. My father said that I was silly to doubt him. (Not to mention greatly disrespectful.) He said that any time an individual migrates to a new world, they do not only bring with them their valuables and material possessions, but they also bring their beliefs and their Gods, their faith and their darkness.

I told him that I still thought he was being a little much. I wish I had listened… I really miss my dog Sparky. He got out the other night and well, he never came back.

Some nights I swear I can hear the Tatamukage outside my walls, the folds of their shadowy limbs popping and crackling like logs in a fireplace. Sometimes I think I see them through the window, beady white eyes peering around the trees… but, I'm probably just being superstitious...

Tooth Picker

DING

A tiny bell jingled above the door as Isaac's father ushered him into the waiting room of the dentist's office. A faceless receptionist welcomed them from behind a small, glass window and told them to have a seat, someone would be with them in a moment. Isaac's eyes darted around the room nervously as they sat down, he kept his mouth shut as tight as possible. His father grabbed a sports magazine from the table and crossed his legs, breathing loudly through his moustache as he thumbed through the pages. Isaac continued to look around until he spotted a small table in the corner with a colorful, wooden bead maze on it. At least there was one thing here that wouldn't be a pain, he thought to himself. He slid out of his chair slowly and started to walk towards the activity center. However, just as he approached the table, the door that separated the waiting room from the dentist's office flung open and a large nurse with a furrowed brow was standing there obtrusively, gripping her clipboard so hard that her knuckles were turning white.

"Isaac!?" she shouted. Which was completely unnecessary since Isaac and his father were the only other people in the waiting room. Isaac looked back at his dad with worried eyes, his father put the magazine down and huffed his way out of the chair. "Go on then." he motioned to the boy. Isaac shook his head no but it only frustrated his father even further. "Boy, you better stop playin' and get in there" he grumbled as he pointed a leathery stub of a finger towards the door. Isaac put his head down and shuffled his feet over to the nurse.

"Go on down the hall, into room #16 and have a seat, Dr. Caliban will be with you soon." said the nurse as she stomped away. Isaac did not like the nurse, she seemed mean and grumpy for no reason. Isaac didn't like anything about the dentist, all the bright lights and tiny metal picks and sharp little tools, even the paper bib they gave him to wear felt cumbersome and bothered him greatly. Everything smelled like rubber and pine and icky, icky medicine. Isaac knew that he had been neglecting his teeth for a long time, he knew that no matter what he did the dentist was going to have to do some *very* intensive work on his nasty teeth and that no matter how gentle they tried to be... it was going to hurt.

After an agonizing fifteen minutes that seemed like forever, Dr. Caliban entered the room. He was tall with perfectly quaffed brown hair and a shiny protruding forehead. Isaac instantly noticed his smile, of course he had a perfect smile, thought Isaac but there was also something about his smile that seemed off. His mouth was so wide and it looked like it was full of one too many teeth, long pearly white teeth like a pristine, freshly painted picket fence was crammed into his mouth. He watched the glare from the overhead lights sparkle on them as the dentist began talking.

"Well hello there young Isaac!" His voice was sing-songy and deep, he spoke with a threatening kindness, "a little bird told me that you are not a big fan of big bad dentists like me, is that true?" he put his hands on his hips and pretended to pout. Isaac closed his mouth even tighter, wrapping his lips all the way around his teeth and nodded "yes" sheepishly.

"Oh, that's quite alright, don't feel bad young sir, you my friend have come to just the right place," Dr. Caliban sat on his stool and rolled over to Isaac's side and whispered out the side of his gigantic mouth, "I don't like other dentists either!" He nudged Isaac with his elbow and winked at him. "Their always so cold and methodical and just so matter of fact," he threw his head back and looked like he was about to unhinge his jaws, "and *so* boring!" He laughed as he looked back at Isaac, "we do things a little different here at Dr. C's... my office is a place where you can feel safe to be yourself and..." he reached into a black medical bag on the floor and pulled out a very old looking ventriloquist dummy, placed it on his lap and made the mouth move, "have *FUN!*" He raised the dolls arms in the air. Isaac did not like the dummy. Its teeth were long and creepy just like Caliban's were. Isaac shook his head side to side, No, no, no! His lips were curled so tight they were beginning to hurt. Dr. Caliban took note of the child's fear and placed the dummy back in its bag.

17

"Hmmm, well it's clear that Mr. Teeth was not the big hit that he usually is, that's ok…" the dentist tapped his foot and pondered for a second looking for another option to help poor Isaac let his guard down. "Ah ha!, he proclaimed suddenly as he reached into the pocket of his coat, "do you like *clowns*, young Isaac?" He pulled out a red rubber nose and placed it over his own, giving it a comical *honk*

"Unh uh!" mouthed Isaac biting his lips and shaking his head again, even harder this time. Isaac hated clowns.

"Ok no clowns." Said Caliban quickly removing the nose and putting it back in his pocket. He crossed his arms and rubbed his chin, "You are a tough one young man. No clowns… no puppetry… hmm.." The doctor looked upon Isaac, trying to figure him out. He eyed him up and down and finally noticed that something had caught Isaac's eye. He followed Isaac's gaze to the office window where he was watching two crows mucking about on a tree branch, he noticed a certain gleam in Isaac's eyes.

"How do you feel about birds Isaac?" Isaac's eyes darted back to Dr. Caliban and a tight-lipped smile spread across his face. "You enjoy them, yes?" Isaac nodded up and down emphatically. Isaac *loved* birds.

"Ah," Dr. Caliban smiled a giant toothy smile, "Well do I have a treat for you young man! Give me just a moment, yes?" Isaac nodded again and the dentist slid out of the room with one long sidestep, disappearing around the corner. Isaac was very excited; he squirmed a little in his seat. He had always adored the innocence and pureness that he saw in the chubby little birds that would hang around his bedroom window and always had respect for the majesty of bigger birds like hawks or eagles. Isaac couldn't wait to see what Dr. C was going to present him next. After a few long minutes Isaac could hear the doctor coming back down the hall, and just before he was standing at the door, he let out a very loud and raucous;

CAW!! CAW!!!

Isaac's heart jumped; he was startled but excited. Caliban entered the room and Isaac let out an audible squeal. There standing before him was Dr. Caliban but in place of the dentist's perfect hair and toothy smile, there was a giant crows head. He cocked his bird head to the side and spoke.

"Do you like my crow mask Isaac?" the beak even opened and closed when he talked. Isaac wasn't sure it was a mask at all, it was so realistic. It had big black feathers that puffed around the neck when the head moved and beady black eyes that blinked. "My friend and patient, Mr. Siboney had it made for me to show his gratitude for saving his life, you see he had an infection in his teeth so bad it was spreading to his brain. I was able to work my magic and in turn Mr. Siboney gifted me this glorious work of art you see before you. It was an ancient ceremonial mask only granted to holy medicine men and shamans, he said that it was only fitting for a doctor such as myself." Dr. Caliban winked at Isaac with the bird's right eye.

Isaac's mouth hung open, and for the first time he spoke, "*So* real…" he said slowly still in awe of Dr. Caliban's magnificent mask.

"Ahhh there they are" said the dentist slowly as he turned his head to look into Isaac's mouth. Isaac shut it again quickly and folded his arms.

"Oh, no need to be afraid my friend," he took a step backwards and put his hands in the air, "we're here to have fun! …Do you know what Mr. Siboney told me to say when I was feeling down? Or when I needed a good laugh?"

Isaac shook his head no.

"He told me to shout as loudly as one can shout;" Caliban tilted his feathered head back and pointed his shiny black beak at the ceiling and shouted, "STI-KI-TI-KI-TEE!! STI-KI-TI-KI-TEEE!!!"

It sounded so ridiculous and so silly that Isaac couldn't help but laugh. He grabbed his stomach and laughed hysterically. Caliban dropped his head and looked directly into Isaac's mouth.

"There they are," The dentist said quickly and quietly. He moved fast, so fast that Isaac didn't notice, Isaac was still laughing his head off. Dr. Caliban's hand reached down and tapped a red button on the wall just behind his back. Suddenly leather straps shot out from beneath the arms of Isaac's chair and wrapped around his wrists, locking them in tightly. Two more straps shout out and locked around his ankles. At the same time, a metal apparatus sprang from behind the head rest and inserted itself into Isaac's mouth prying it open and keeping his mouth frozen and teeth completely exposed. Isaac tried to move, he tried to scream, he could do neither.

The bird doctor clucked his beak disappointedly at Isaac, "Tut, tut, young friend… you have not been brushing one single bit now have you?" He walked slowly to Isaac's side and peered down at his open mouth, "disgusting." His S's hissed and every syllable was sharp. Caliban ran his fingers over the shiny metal tools laying neatly on the tray next to Isaac's shoulder, "had you not been such a naughty boy and simply taken care of those precious pearly bones in your mouth, we wouldn't be in this predicament would we?" he turned to look over his shoulder at Isaac who was trying to break free from the straps with all his might, "try anything funny and I'll use my shiny little friends here to cut ALL your teeth out!"

Isaac was no longer having any fun. He was terrified and shaking, tears were rolling down his cheeks and saliva was dripping down his chin. Dr. Caliban sat down on his rolling stool and slid himself right next to Isaac's ensnared cranium. "Now now," he started, "no need to cry young Isaac. We reap what we sow and I bet you'd sew your own mouth shut if you could right now wouldn't you?" Isaac didn't even know what that was supposed to mean, all he knew was that he wanted to be absolutely anywhere other than where he was at the moment. He cried and he tried to scream but his throat was too dry, all he could make out was a gurgling whimper. Caliban inched closer. "Now... let's start with that CAW-Corrupted canine!" and in a flash of black feathers, the doctor lunged forward with his beak in a breakneck pecking motion. Caliban closed his beak on the tooth and ripped it right out of Isaac's mouth with sheer force. He threw his head back and swallowed the tooth into his mask and let out a series of loud caws, puffing out all of his feathers.

Somewhere in the waiting room, over the mellow jazz music playing quietly from the speakers in the ceiling, Isaac's dad looked up from his sporting magazine and scratched his head. What was that noise he wondered, it sounded like someone let a whole murder of crows into the back office? He shook his head at such a silly idea and went back to a particularly droll article about fly fishing in Patagonia.

Back in Operating Room 16, Isaac writhed under the straps of Caliban's torturous contraption. He was whimpering and sobbing uncontrollably. Caliban cocked his giant crow head to the side and looked at the boy, "Hey, I thought we were having fun! Remember? Sti-ki-stiki-tee! No?"

Isaac shook his head "No" as much as he could with his limited mobility. "Oh, come on" urged the wicked dentist, "Stiki-stiki-teee!" He bent forward and started inching closer to Isaac's face, his voice getting louder and more furious with every step, "STIKI-STINKY-TEE!" He was practically breathing down Isaacs open mouth at this point, "STINKY, STINKY TEETH!" He screamed, "STINKY STINKY STINKY TEETH!!!" Caliban bellowed at the boy as he picked another tooth out of his mouth and swallowed it down.

This time the boy's father was sure he had heard something strange coming from the back. He put down the magazine, walked over to the reception area, and knocked on the tiny piece of glass. For a while the window didn't budge at all, and he could still hear a faint cacophony of weird sounds. The noise rose and fell in volume and continued to get stranger and stranger, finally there was a loud metal crash and what sounded like many objects falling to the floor. Isaac's father really hoped that his son wasn't back there causing trouble for the dentist. He knocked again and after a few more moments the beveled glass slid to the side and the burly nurse was frowning at him, her rectangular face almost perfectly framed by the window box. "Yes?"

"Sorry to bother, uh, ma'am... Do you have a- um, a bird loose inside of your building? Because I keep hearing-"

"Sir, with all due respect, that is ridiculous."

"I know it is, I know but see, I've been hearing-"

"Oh look," said the nurse as she looked back over her shoulder, "here comes your boy now.

Unable to see around the nurse's car-engine-sized head, Isaac's father stepped over to the doorway and waited for his son on the other side. The door opened slowly and revealed Dr. Caliban, back to his normal self with his very normal hair and terrible smile standing next to a very dazed and shaken Isaac. Isaac's head was wrapped with a white cloth that held an ice pack by his jaw. His olive cheeks had blotchy patches of Rosie red skin. His eyes were wide and glossed over.

"How'd uh, how did everything go boy?"

Isaac looked up at his father with watery eyes and opened his mouth to speak but was unable to do so, his jaw was wired shut. His hand flew up to rub his cheek as he winced in pain.

"Oh, I'm afraid young Isaac here won't be able to talk for quite some time. He had quite the job for me!" Chuckled Caliban as he put his hands on Isaac's shoulders. He put his hand to the side of his mouth and leaned forward to whisper to his dad, "oh and... he may be a little out of it as well, such an enormous amount of dentistry called for quite a bit of heavy anesthetics so he might speak of... hallucinations when he does regain his speech. Just be wary, and regale his stories no matter how far-fetched they might seem."

23

"Right..." said his father eyeing his son, "come on son, let's get you home then. Get you some rest."

They said their goodbyes, paid an outrageously hefty bill, and left Dr. Caliban's office. Isaac was so traumatized he could barely think. He trudged along as his father pulled him to the car. Would anyone even believe his story? When would he be able to speak? Isaac wasn't even sure he wanted to, the only thing he was sure of was that he would never neglect his teeth again and that he didn't care if he ever saw another bird.

Old Crinkle Bones

Legend has it, if you ever happen to go play down by the creek, and you stumble upon a cave with a crinkly, crooked little man standing in front of it, you should immediately turn around and run back home as fast as you can. Run back to your parent or guardian and hug them tight and forget you ever even saw that jagged, jangly person by the cave. If, however, you were not wise enough to turn tail and run, and you happen to be so unlucky as to engage that gangly gremlin of a man in conversation... be sure to never tell him your name. Protect your name from him at all costs! Now, if you ever actually find yourself trapped in conversation with Old Crinkle Bones, and he tricks you into playing his "Game of Names" well then, all you can really do is cross your fingers, hold your breath, and pray for your sake that he *never* guesses your name correctly. For if he does guess your name, and he gets it right, well then he gets your soul and when your soul belongs to Crinkle Bones your body becomes empty, and cursed. Many children in the neighborhood who have fallen victim to such an ill fate have disappeared entirely. Many have come home to their parents only, never quite the same. Those who come home are hollow and lifeless, they walk around like zombies and slowly but surely, one by one their bones begin to crinkle up. Arms bend backwards, knees become inverted, necks turn sideways, and their heads hang upside down as they crawl around like giant fleshy spiders. Truly an unsettling sight to see indeed. Perhaps you would be well advised to in fact never play down by the creek at all. It can be quite a dangerous place. The children even have a song about it;

Down by the creek there's a cave, there's a cave.
Where the children go to play,
go to play, go to play
And Crinkle Bones, calls it hoooome.

Old Crinkle Bones has a game, has a game.
Let the old man guess your name, guess your name
and if he gets it right
then he gets to take your sooooul.

And aaaaalll your boooones will CRINKLE UP!

CRINKLE.

CRACKLE.

SNAP!

BAD MOON

On a cold January night in 1972, best friends Alex and Tommy ran down the street towards the house of their other best friend, Farrah. They could not wait to tell her about what their parents had told them earlier that night. What their parents had told them was one of the creepiest things that had happened in their town, or at least near their town, in as long as they could remember; and Farrah, Alex, & Tommy, *loved* all things creepy. The street was covered in a thick fog, it was dark and chilly but not cold enough to snow. Winter had not quite hit town just yet. They ran up the stairs of Farrah's front porch, flung open the screen door and both knocked on the front door at the same time as many times as they could before Farrah's mother opened the door.

"Alright, alright boys! Enough. Keep it up and you'll wear the paint right off the poor door!" she ushered them inside and helped them take off their coats. "Farrah sweety!" She called over her shoulder, "the boys are here!"

Farrah came bounding down the stairs and stopped halfway.

"Hey guys! Come on up! I got the newest issue of Troubling Tales! It's SO good!"

"OK but first, you're not gonna believe what happened!" said Tommy excitedly as he ran to the stairs. Alex was right behind him.

"It is so gross, and so creepy!" huffed Alex between breaths as they all climbed to the second floor.

Farrah raised one of her eyebrows as she opened the sticker covered door to her room letting the boys in.

"Is it grosser than Mrs. Paisley's blood boils?"

"*Way* grosser!" said Alex as he plopped down on Farrah's bed.

"Creepier than the whistling window in Alex's hallway bathroom?" asked Farrah, turning around the wooden chair at her desk and sitting on it backwards.

"*Way* creepier!" said Tommy.

"What?" exclaimed Alex, "Nothing is creepier than my hallway bathroom! I wish we never did Bloody Mary in there… it's been cursed ever since."

"Nah, It's not cursed, you're just scared!" Tommy teased

"It is too! and I am not!" Alex shot back as he nudged Tommy's shoulder

"Boys! Focus! Either spill the beans or give me the floor so I can show you guys the new Troubling Tales! This thing is *full* of creepy." said Farrah holding up the newest issue. The cover showing some sort of demon with bat wings standing over a feasting vampire.

Tommy turned his head slowly towards Farrah, "Oh, we've got your creepy, and it is so much more than a stupid magazine… Do you remember Mr. Hemlock?"

Farrah turned her head to the side trying to recall the name. "I don't think so, sounds kind of familiar though, and Troubling Tales is *not* stupid thank you very much."

"Well he used to teach AP Science at the high school, everyone that ever had him always said how he was like the meanest teacher that ever lived, hated kids, hated everyone really and people could hear him yelling at his students from three classrooms down."

Alex jumped in, "they say that the only time he ever seemed happy was when he was teaching astronomy, like

stars and planets and stuff, but even then, if you got
something wrong…he would just like, lose his freaking mind
I guess."

"Why teach kids if you hate them so much?" asked Farrah.

"Go figure," said Tommy, "but one day, like five years
ago, he just had enough and he just up and quit his job and
then totally disappeared. Didn't tell anyone where he was
going, he had no family or relatives or nothin' so there was no
way of even tracking him. He just left."

"Yeah, he hated everyone so much that he went and
moved to a house in the middle of the forest where nobody
could find him!" Alex chimed in again.

Tommy whacked Alex on the shoulder with the back of
his hand. "I was getting there! Jeez, you have no idea how to
build up a good story I swear."

Alex rubbed his shoulder and looked at the floor, "sorry
jeez…"

"Don't be a jerk Tommy" said Farrah.

"Just let me finish ok?" Tommy rubbed his hands together,
"This is where the story gets good. So, he moves to the
woods, right? No one there, no one for miles around. He gets
so much food and water and stuff that he doesn't even need to
leave to go to market ever. 'Cause y'know, he doesn't want to
deal with those people either. It's just him, his radio, his house
and the woods. Oh, and his star charts."

"Yeah like I said," Alex jumped in, "guy was obsessed
with astronomy."

"Yeah, right. So, he's there in his cabin and he's not doing
anything besides listening to his radio and charting the stars
and never having to hear anything from anybody. Here's the
thing though, Mr. Hemlock was *super* old right? He's got a
real bad heart and no medicine and no one to take him to the

hospital out in the woods, so after being out in the sticks for so long by himself, his heart just gives out. Old Hemlock has a heart attack in his favorite easy chair and dies rotten and alone."

"He didn't have a phone line or something? Like, he knew that he had a bad heart, didn't he? Why didn't he call when he needed help?" asked Farrah.

"No phones. No tv. His only connection to the outside world was an old transistor radio and it wasn't a two way." answered Tommy

"I don't think he wanted any help. Maybe he kind of *wanted* to die." Alex said as he stared at his hands.

"Probably." said Tommy, "and get this… Mr. Hemlock died *two years* ago. His body wasn't found until some hiker was exploring the woods about a week ago! His body was being preserved by the maggots and all the junk he was surrounded by in his house this whole time! When they found him, he was basically a mummified corpse!"

"Whoa." was all Farrah could get out.

Alex looked up at Farrah, "Yeah they said his body was like just all black and kind of purple except for these white rings around his eye sockets and there were flies and maggots everywhere. They also said his lips were just gone, probably eaten by the bugs, so you could see all of his yellow teeth like a skeleton. One of the police guys told my dad's friend Bill, that the smell was so bad he threw up immediately, before he even got into the house."

Farrah's mouth was hanging open. "That is so… *so* gross."

"The best part though," A wide grin spread across Tommy's face, "guess which woods his hideaway house was in?"

"Evergrove?" asked Farrah.

"Nope. Redgrove."

Farrah's eyes got wide and a little glossy "No."

"Yes," Tommy's grin was almost too wide for his face now. "Right behind your house! I mean, it's way way deep in there but it's in the woods that start right behind your neighborhood! You know what this means right? Right?"

"I don't know Tommy." Alex said sheepishly

Tommy couldn't stop himself from talking at this point, he was almost too excited "and, And! Rumor has it, the last thing he wrote before he died, in his little star chart journal thing, He said that on January 25th of this year, there is going to be a blood moon!"

"A what? Is that an actual thing?" asked Farrah. "I mean, don't get me wrong that sounds super cool and super creepy but, what does that mean?"

"I don't know, the guy was a kook but the 25th..."

"That's tomorrow." said Alex.

"Tomorrow night my fine friends. And *we* are going to investigate. Underneath the blood moo-o-o-o-n." Tommy dragged out the last word in his deepest voice and wiggled his fingers at Alex.

Alex was not sure that was a very sound idea. "Isn't that like a crime scene or something now? What if there's cops?"

"There won't be any cops you dingbat. There was no crime to make it a crime scene. The guy just died. They took his body, now the place is condemned. Which means we," Tommy motioned to the three of them, "can snoop around and see just how creepy this place really is. Maybe find some cool knick knacks to add to Fairy's collection" gesturing over his

31

shoulder to one of Farrah's shelves where she had one small porcelain clown, one dirty old rag doll, two different gemstones and one brass antique necklace, all found from different abandoned and spooky places they had previously explored. Farrah's favorite was the porcelain clown, they had found it in an old abandoned mansion in the next town over.

Farrah rolled her eyes at Tommy "Please stop calling me Fairy."

"But you used to love being called Fairy," said Alex as he got up and meandered over to Farrah's knick knack shelf, running his finger over the old rag doll. The doll creeped him out but for some reason he was always drawn to it.

"Uh yeah, when we were in second grade," said Farrah incredulously, "anyways… I'm in."

Alex shot a glance to Farrah over his shoulder, he knew that if the two of them were set on going then he would have no choice. "Really?"

"Yeah," she shrugged and looked out her window to the foggy woods behind her house "could be fun. Plus, that whole blood moon thing is very interesting."

"Then it's set," said Tommy standing up from the bed "Tomorrow night, we meet up here. I'll bring the flashlight, Alex grab your map and your compass, Fairy bring your baseball bat. We'll meet around 5 and head out a little bit before it gets dark. Deal?"

"Deal." Farrah stood up and dropped her magazine on her desk, who needs spooky stories when we can write our own, she thought.

Alex put Farrah's doll back on the shelf and turned around to face the other two. He looked up at the ceiling and let out a deep sigh. "Ugh. Fine. Deal."

"Hands in. Shadow Squad motto." said Farrah, holding her hand out flat in the air. Tommy put his hand flat on top of hers and Alex put his hand on top of Tommy's.

The three of them chanted in chorus,
"From light comes shadow,
And in the shadows we'll find,
The deepest and darkest,
Of the secrets we hide."

"I still don't really get the motto." said Alex as he put his hand back in his pocket.

"It's just some cool poem Farrah found in one of those scary story magazines." replied Tommy "plus it goes with the name of our crew, we are the Shadow Squad, right? We're like the gang from Scooby Doo only we don't have the dog."

"It's not *just* to sound cool," Farrah retorted as she sat back down and picked up her issue of Troubling Tales, thumbing through the pages, "It's deeper than that. It means that even in places of light and happiness we can find darkness and mystery, and in the darkest shadows we know we can find even more than what scares us, we can find excitement and adventure and something new," she eyed her shelf of trinkets, "And it means we are brave enough to face that darkness and explore those shadows. Everything else has been so figured out by adults and scientists and stuff. This is like the last frontier for us."

Alex smiled. Farrah's speeches always made him feel braver than he really was. For a girl that was so into darkness she sure had a bright personality. Alex liked that, he knew Tommy did too, it's the reason that Farrah was the real leader of the group, no matter how many times Tommy said otherwise.

The Shadow Squad converged on the floor of Farrah's room and looked over the Troubling Tales magazine, sharing stories and ogling the vibrant illustrations for about an hour or so. They laughed and discussed what they thought would happen on their next adventure until they all started to get tired. At one-point Alex almost fell asleep on the floor. Tommy nudged Alex on the shoulder, "Come on sleepy head, your mom's probably worried sick already. Let's get you back home."

His mother would indeed be worried but Alex's mom was never really *not* worried, he was used to it. Alex knew the real reason Tommy wanted to leave so early was because Tommy was afraid of what his father would say, or do, if he came home a minute too late but Alex would never bring that up.

"Yeah, you're right, let's go. See you tomorrow Farrah, thanks for showing us the new issue, I really dug it. Maybe uh, maybe I could borrow it some time?"

Farrah brushed her hair behind her ear, "oh yeah, totally. See you guys. Get home safe."

"See ya Fairy." teased Tommy as he ran out of her room before she could throw any stuffed animals or books at him.

The boys returned into the foggy night and headed back home.

*****

The very next night, around 5pm at Farrah's house, the trio met up just like they had planned. The Shadow Squad assembled themselves in Farrah's backyard and prepared for the night's adventure. It was still light out but the sun would be setting in a few hours. The daylight seemed soft and slightly more red than usual, the sky had a few scattered lumpy clouds but was otherwise clear. The air was crisp and a little chilly. Luckily, they all dressed accordingly. Alex was carefully organizing snack foods and placing it into his backpack. Tommy pulled some extra flashlight batteries from his pocket and handed them to Alex,

"Here, stuff these in there too, just in case we run out."

Farrah was switching between practicing her swing with her brother's baseball bat and passively watching the sky. Alex pulled out his map and zipped up his backpack.

"Ready?" asked Tommy.

"Ready." Farrah and Alex replied in unison.

The three friends headed off into the forest.

"Alright," said Alex holding up his map as he walked, "my Dad's friend told me that it was almost to the edge of the forest near the Quarry and somewhere not far off the Redgrove hiking trail so..."

Alex adjusted the map and took care to watch his step, he didn't want to accidently trip over a large rock in his path.

"So that means, it's gotta be somewhere... "he circled a small area on the map with his finger, "right around here."

Farrah looked over his shoulder to see where he was pointing, "That's probably only about a mile or so that way" she said pointing to the west.

"We'll be there in no time," said Tommy with a smile and a stride in his step.

After about an hour of walking Tommy was starting to wonder if they were getting lost. There were so many trees and rocks and bushes that everything was starting to look the same.

"You sure that compass works Slick?" Tommy asked as he threw a rock in no particular direction.

Alex was annoyed and frustrated with Tommy's insufferable attitude. Normally he didn't mind but for the past 10 minutes Alex had an inexplicable urge to turn and scream at Tommy till his face turned blue.

"The compass works fine." He said shortly.

"I don't know dude," Tommy kept at it, "starting to feel a little lost out here... I think I've seen that same tree before."

"We're not lost," Farrah piped up, "we're close, I can feel it."

Farrah pointed at a clearing in the brush, "Look, that's the Redgrove Hiking Trail! That means the house should be somewhere..."

"There."

Alex had stopped dead in his tracks. He was pointing straight ahead towards a dense thicket of trees. Through the trees, the three could just make out the wooden paneling on the side of what had to be Hemlock's house.

"Wicked." said Tommy

"Far out." said Farrah

"Let's just go." said Alex as he marched forward towards the hidden house.

Farrah caught up to Alex and walked next to him, trying to keep pace but he was almost speed walking at this point.

"Hey man, are you Ok? Why are you in such a hurry all of a sudden?"

Alex started to fold up the map as he walked, crushing the edges and smashing it together haphazardly. Now Farrah *really* knew something was wrong. Alex was very particular about keeping his things nice and neat and had never once folded a piece of paper without being as gentle as possible. She grabbed him by the shoulder and stopped him in his tracks.

"Alex! What is your deal man?"

Alex scowled and jolted his shoulder away from Farrah's hand violently. Farrah flinched and pulled her hand back. Alex saw the hurt in her face. She looked like a scared animal, like Tommy's dog when anyone reached out to pet her. Alex never wanted to make Farrah feel that way. To be completely honest Alex didn't even know why he was acting out. Ever since they got close to the house, he had felt this wave of anger and fury wash over him and he couldn't explain why or where it came from. He shook his head and wiped his face with his hands.

"I'm so sorry. I can't- I don't... I don't know why I did that. I don't know what came over me. Something about this place-"

"It's ok," Farrah interrupted, "I know, I felt it too." she looked around the area surrounding the house, "it's like the air in this place is just stained with Hemlock's anger... all that hatred."

"Yeah," Alex agreed pushing up one of his backpack straps and looking up at the house, "totally."

Tommy, who had been lagging a bit behind, caught up and breezed past the two of them.

"Come on Squad! Mystery awaits!

Tommy bounded right up to the front of Hemlock's house. Farrah and Alex followed right behind, the three of them stopped at the foot of the porch stairway.

"Ok," Alex gulped, "this is real now."

"Dig it." Said Farrah dreamily.

The cabin was only two stories tall but standing in front of it, it felt like it was towering over the three friends. The building itself seemed modern, like it had been plucked right out of their neighborhood and planted in the middle of the forest but the rot in the wood and the growing moss and weeds that were overtaking the thing made it feel ancient.

"Does it look *off* to you guys?" asked Tommy pacing towards the corner of the house, eyeing the alignment of the structure.

"Like, how do you mean? Because this whole trip feels off to me man. This place has a bad energy."

"Bad smell too." said Farrah, pinching her nose.

"No not like that kinda off, like… doesn't the whole thing look kind of... crooked?" said Tommy rejoining the group and standing at the front again.

All three of them tilted their heads to the side at the same time.

"Huh," Farrah scrunched her nose while keeping her head tilted, "I think so... but it's hard to tell," she said slowly.

Alex cocked his head back up and shook off the jitters he was getting from all of this, "Let's do it. Let's just get this over with. This place gives me the willies something fierce."

Tommy turned to Alex, "Hey man, I know I'm tough on you about this stuff sometimes but, I don't really mean it. If you don't want to do this we can turn back now."

Farrah looked at Tommy with doe-eyes then back to Alex, "Yeah, hey, we totally do not need to go in there. I mean we found the place, already right? At least we know the story is real and-"

"No. I want to do this." Alex stopped Farrah, "I mean we're already here, let's see what we find… let's just make it fast yeah?" he half smiled.

Farrah beamed at Alex, "Yeah."

Tommy ruffled Alex's hair and took his first steps up to the porch of Hemlock's cabin. Alex and Farrah followed close behind. The floorboards on the porch groaned with each step. The three of them walked tightly together and stopped at the door.

"Here goes nothing," whispered Tommy as he turned the door knob and pushed it open. The door swung slowly and creaked loudly, the sun was starting to go down and it was hard to see but they could make out piles and piles of trash. They were immediately hit by the smell of death and hot garbage.

"Oh, it reeks!" yelped Tommy as he covered his nose and mouth.

"Shhhhh!" hushed Alex and Farrah at the same time.

"For what?" Tommy laughed through his cupped hand, "I uh, I don't think anybody's home." he motioned to the barren wasteland inside the cabin with his flashlight.

"Whatever." Farrah shoved passed Tommy and into the house. She pulled the bandana out of her hair and wrapped it around the lower half of her face to help cover the smell. The boys both pulled their shirts over their noses and followed her in. Tommy turned on his flashlight and scanned the inside of the house.

The main room of the cabin was a canyon made of garbage; hundreds of old beer bottles, water bottles, and soda cans. There were smatterings of microwave dinner trays and empty cereal boxes. Somewhere on the left side of the room underneath everything they could just make out a couch that looked like it had only ever been used as a place to store extra trash. Towards the back of the room along the back wall was the kitchen area. The sink was cascading with dirty dishes. The walls and cupboards were splattered with some sort of crusty brown and orange goo. On the left side there was an open doorway leading to a bedroom 'If you could call that a bedroom' thought Farrah. From what they could see there was one plain mattress on the floor covered only by ominous brown stains and a couple crushed soda cans. Next to the mattress was an old lamp with a stained-glass shade and a couple rows of open jugs and cups, all filled with dark yellow liquid. Tommy moved the flashlight to a spot on the living room wall and nudged Alex's sides with his elbow.

"Dig it," his flashlight illuminated giant red letters scrawled over the wallpaper.

KEEP YOUR EYES IN THE SKY

"What was this guy on about..." muttered Alex.

"Look, I think he wrote on this wall too," said Farrah tapping Tommy's shoulder, "give me some light over here."

Tommy moved the flashlight to the adjacent wall and sure enough there were more red letters scribbled on the wall.

FOLLOW THE STARS.
FALL TO THE MOON.

"What a creep," said Tommy, "you think he did it with his own blood?"

"No way," Alex shot back quickly, "it's too bright, if it was blood it would have turned brown by now."

Farrah edged a little closer to get a better look, "I think it's chalk," she touched the corner of the letter N and a smudge of red chalk stuck to her finger, "yup. Red chalk." she showed her finger to the boys.

"You're nuts." laughed Tommy, "I can't believe you touched that stuff."

"Yeah Farrah," added Alex, "just to be safe I wouldn't touch like, anything in this place. Who knows what-"

"Oh please!" Farrah shouted, "would you two stop being such babies!"

She pushed past them both and stomped towards the staircase leading up to the second story loft and looked up.

"You guys coming or what?" Farrah asked coldly, holding her baseball bat over one shoulder and tapping her right foot.

Alex walked over to Farrah and looked her in the eyes. For a second he swore he saw a flash of red gleam across them. He outstretched his hand and put it on her shoulder.

"Hey, remember what happened to me outside? Don't let this place get to you."

Farrah stared back at Alex. She wanted to wipe the smug look off of his face, she wanted to grab his hand off of her shoulder and yank his arm right out of its socket. She imagined how he'd look after she did it, yelping in pain… but his face, in her mind it looked so sad, so hurt. That's not what she wanted. She never wanted to hurt Alex or Tommy or ever break the trust they had in her. It had to be the hatred brooding in this evil place, she thought. She could feel it trying to crawl inside of her brain and take control. She had to shake it off. Farrah looked back to Alex's face and snapped out of it. She clasped her hand over her mouth.

"I'm so sorry!" she put her hand on Alex's, "we really have to be careful. We can't let whatever darkness that's lurking here take control of us. Any of us." she said sternly as she turned to look at Tommy.

Alex agreed, Tommy shrugged it off.

"You guys are really letting this stuff get to your head," he said as he broke the two up and proceeded to walk up the stairs, talking to them over his shoulder, "No more Troubling Tales for you two. Come on, let's check out the loft."

Alex and Farrah looked at each other and both rolled their eyes. Tommy's voice came echoing down the stairway.

"Whoa… double whoa! Guys!" he called, "You have to… have to see this..." he trailed off.

They quickly shot up the stairs to the loft.

As soon as they reached the second floor, they were struck by two things; the first thing was the view from the giant glass pane windows on the opposite side of the room. The windows ran from the floor to the a-frame ceiling and beyond them was an astonishing panoramic view of the treetops of the forest and the striking skyline above. It was twilight, the sun was almost done setting and the sky was a gradient shade of glowing cyan fading into a deep royal blue that ultimately swirled into an inky black night freckled with white stars. The clouds were still slightly pink and purple from the few rays of sunset that were lingering behind. Farrah let out an audible gasp, she was in awe.

The second thing that struck them was the same thing that had apparently struck Tommy as well. Tommy was frozen in place, staring at an old, rotting easy chair.

Alex, who had been so caught up in the view that he hadn't even noticed the latter until he looked at Tommy, dropped his face when he followed Tommy's gaze to the decrepit piece of furniture.

"Is that the spot where he," Alex gulped, "died?"

Farrah turned to look at the chair, "oh man." she let out.

"Of course, it is." Said Tommy shortly, unmoving from his slightly hunched over stance, swallowing the image of the chair with his eyes.

"That is, *crazy,*" said Alex, "look at the back of it, you can literally see the spot where his head was laying back and rotting away. Look at the arms too! The whole thing is still indented from his body." .

"So gnarly." said Tommy quietly.

Farrah looked at the chair then back to the windows.

"And look, he positioned it perfectly to keep his 'eyes in the sky'." she said softly as she gazed out towards the gigantic moon that was now visible through the window. "Now *that,* is far out man, check out the moon! It's pink! Like, it really is turning blood red that's insa-"

BOOM!

There was a crash like thunder. All three of them froze in place.

"That came from inside the house," whispered Farrah.

"Downstairs." muttered Alex.

Tommy snapped out of his frozen state and scowled at the stairs, "It's probably some stupid teenagers, trying to rile us up." each word came out more furious than the last. He rushed past Alex, "Give me the bat," he spat through gritted teeth as he grabbed the bat out of Farrah's hands without pause.

"Tommy wait!" Farrah hissed.

It was no use, Tommy was already halfway down the stairs, bat in one hand, flashlight in the other, and seething at the mouth.

"You think you can scare us!?" Shouted Tommy waving the bat and shining the flashlight in every direction possible.

Farrah and Alex carefully crept down the stairs behind Tommy.

"Huh!?" Tommy continued to shout, "Come on out you cowards!"

BOOM.

Another crash. This time it was clear that it came from the bedroom. Tommy whipped around and shined the flashlight on the bedroom doorway. There, standing in the door's frame, was a towering, rotting Mr. Hemlock.

"Hemlock," whispered Alex.

His once pale skin was dark and leathered, like a skeleton wrapped in beef jerky. There were white rings around his eyes but the sockets were completely empty, as if the eyeballs were clawed out of his skull. His lips were completely peeled back and two rows of long brown and yellow teeth were exposed. Still draped in the old ragged flannel shirt and holey jeans he died in; Hemlock's stinking corpse loomed in the hallway. He let out a low gravely moan and then suddenly lurched forward with his hands outstretched towards Farrah, Tommy and Alex.

The three friends wasted no time. Farrah and Alex immediately ran to the left towards the front door of the cabin. Tommy turned tail and jolted up the stairs to the loft. They didn't expect a dead body to move so fast but Hemlock was gaining on them quickly. Alex looked over his shoulder and tried to yell out to Tommy but all he could get out was, "Whatya-Ahhh!" before Farrah yanked on his jacket collar and pulled him through the doorway.

Farrah and Alex had made it outside, they jumped off of the porch and ran for 50 feet into the dark of the forest before they stopped and look back.

"Is- huh-he- Is, he gone?" Alex wheezed in between gasping breaths.

Farrah held onto her knees and looked back at the house, "I think... he went... for Tommy" she panted.

44

"Awe jeez," lamented Alex, "what do we do? We can't just leave him in there? Can we?"

"No," huffed Farrah as she stood up and caught her breath, "Friends don't leave friends behind."

It was dark outside but the moon was so bright they could see everything around them. There was a low layer of fog on the ground and the air felt like cold steel against their skin. The forest was painfully quiet.

Alex looked at the cabin, it was only a quick jog away but it felt like he was staring down an endless hallway, he was getting dizzy just thinking about it. He looked back at Farrah

"Ok, well, we need to like, think of a plan or something. We can't just rush in there; Tommy still has the bat *and* the flashlight. We have… a map, three sandwiches, one red pen, and a compass." said Alex as he threw his hands up.

"Alex! We do not have time to sit out here and make a plan or take inventory! Tommy is still in there with that- *that thing*!" shouted Farrah as she paced back and forth, "give me the pen!"

"What? What are you going to do with a pen?" Alex asked as he fumbled with his backpack trying desperately to find it.

"I don't know Alex! But it's better than sitting here, doing *nothing*." replied Farrah growing more anxious by the second, "ugh, just, please give me the bag!"

Alex threw the backpack to Farrah, she rummaged around for a few seconds and found the pen almost immediately, she threw the backpack back to Alex and started back towards the house, brandishing the red pen like a knife.

"I just-just really think we should have a plan," Alex shouted at Farrah's back, "Farrah!"

"There's no time Alex," said Farrah as she whipped around.

"How do we stop a freaking zombie?" asked Alex exasperated.

Alex looked to Farrah for a reply but Farrah just stood there, staring at him with glossy eyes.

"Farrah?"

"Alex." Farrah said quietly.

"Is he even a zombie? A mummy I guess tech-" Alex stopped when he saw Farrah put her hand up in the air.

"Alex."

"What's wrong?"

"Alex. Run."

Alex suddenly felt a deep wave of dread wash over him. He didn't need to turn around to know that somehow, Hemlock had suddenly appeared behind him. Alex could feel Hemlock's furious anger permeating the night air around them, like standing in front of a baking oven. It made him sweat and gave him the chills at the same time. For a moment he was frozen, until he heard Farrah's voice cutting through fog in his brain.

"RUN!!!" she screamed

Alex snapped out of it and he and Farrah both took off as fast as they possibly could. They could hear him close behind, dragging his dead feet through the leaves on the ground at an abnormally fast pace, *shhkt, shhkt, shhkt, shhkt!* They leapt up the stairs of the porch and burst through the front door, back into the house. "Tommy!?" Farrah shouted as she scrambled around a corner and dashed towards the staircase. Alex was one step behind her. They both came to a holt at the bottom of the stairs when a flash of blinding white light hit them in the face. It was Tommy. He was standing at the top of the stairs holding out his flashlight in his left hand and letting the baseball bat drag on the ground with his right.

"Tommy it's us!" exclaimed Farrah as she crossed her arms over face to block the light from her eyes. Alex turned his head to shield his face from the light as well but as he started to regain his eyesight, he saw a silhouette starting to form in the front doorway of the house, "Guys," Alex's voice was shaking, "He's here!"

Tommy moved the flashlight from his friends to the door. Hemlocks corpse was illuminated and all of his grotesque features were staring the trio in the face. Alex could now see the maggots crawling in and out of the cavities in Hemlock's body. Farrah took one look at Hemlock and started to dash up the stairs but before she even set her foot back down Tommy took one long, deep, rattling breath and let out one of the loudest voices they had ever heard.

"LEAVE!!!"

The word boomed out of Tommy's voice box like a wrecking ball smashing through a brick wall. It was so loud and so strong that it shook the walls of the cabin and literally knocked Farrah and Alex backwards. Farrah fell on top of Alex and Alex was sent crashing to the floor. They both looked up in a stupor to see Hemlock's body getting shattered by the soundwave. The mummified zombie who had seemed so hulking and menacing moments ago, just exploded into dust and ash and blew away into the night sky.

"Whoah." Alex mouthed the word but no sound actually came out. Farrah got up and dusted herself off looking up at Tommy, "How did you do that? How did you know to do that?"

Alex got up slowly, "Yeah man, that was *insane*." he laughed. Farrah started to climb the stairs toward him.

"I said, leave." Tommy spat sternly.

Farrah stopped in her tracks and locked eyes with him, the whites of his eyes were blazing red, his pupils were flickering like a lantern.

"Tommy, listen to me very carefully," Farrah started, "this place has a hold of you, it's trying to turn you like it did to Mr. Hemlock. We need to get you out of here. You're going to be fine we just, we just really need to get out of this terrible place."

Tommy slowly tilted his head back towards the ceiling and in a low voice that almost sounded like two people speaking at once he uttered, "...the stars are mine and mine alone, I am for the moon... and tonight, we will all be consumed..."

"Tommy please!" Farrah's voice cracked and her eyes started to well up with tears.

Tommy snapped his head back down and locked eyes with her again. His gaze intensified, his head began to shake, his entire body was vibrating. Alex and Farrah could both feel the vibrations running through the house and in their heads, it blurred their vision and made their ears ring. Farrah stepped backwards down the stairs slowly as she looked at Tommy, terrified and heart broken.

"That's not you..." She muttered quietly. Tears rolled down her cheeks as she reached the bottom of the stairs and grabbed Alex's hand, "That's not our Tommy..."

"I know," said Alex as he placed his other hand on Farrah's shoulder. Tears were streaming down his face too. He was even more afraid of Tommy than he was of seeing Mr. Hemlock. Something about his presence was ferociously threatening, it was like he was exhaling pure evil and those eyes... Those eyes looked like Tommy could cut through the walls if he wanted too.

"We have to get help." Alex declared, "we can't save Tommy alone. Whatever's got his claws in him is in there deep."

Farrah nodded. "We're coming back for you Tommy Landers! We are getting help and we are coming back!" she pointed her finger at him as she backed away.

"Fairy?" Tommy said in a weak voice.

Farrah stopped and looked back at Tommy, she gripped Alex's hand as tight as she could, was the real Tommy coming through?

"Tommy?" her voice wavered slightly

Tommy snapped his head to the side and grinned that evil grin, "Run!" he growled.

The house shook and something in the walls made a deafening cracking noise. Farrah turned and darted through the door hand in hand with Alex. The two ran through the forest and didn't stop until they reached the edge, they didn't look at the compass or the map, they weren't even sure they were heading in the right direction but they didn't stop running until they knew they were out of the forest and out of danger.

When they got home, they told their parents everything, even the parts they both knew their parents would never believe. They repeated the same story to the police and all their other friends and neighbors over and over until they were sick of it. They brought them back to the cabin that night but there was no sign of Tommy or Hemlock anywhere. The town organized massive search parties, the first night the fog surrounding the forest was so thick, they almost had to call it off. The fog had dissipated by the second night, but it was no matter, no one ever found Tommy Landers. The only trace they ever found were two chalky red handprints on the glass windows and a new sentence written in red chalk on the walls in the loft of Hemlock's cabin;

I WILL BE WATCHING
I'LL SEE YOU SOON
FROM FAR AWAY
ATOP THE MOON

*****

To this very day, Alex and Farrah remain haunted by the memory of their dear lost friend. Haunted by the horrible visions of Hemlock, lodged in their brains. Haunted by everything that happened that night, under the blood moon, in Redgrove Forest.

Alex never stepped near another forest again. His family moved to another state, to a big city, where they replaced the trees and rolling hills with skyscrapers and shopping malls. Alex does his best to keep himself and his mind busy. But every once in a while, when the city lights are just dim enough to see the stars in the sky, Alex thinks back to that night and he freezes with fear. As if the stars were watching and just waiting for him to make the wrong move.

Farrah sees it in the moon. She stuck around town and the stigma stayed with her. From the day they came home, the two of them were labeled the prime suspects in the disappearance of Tommy. Never enough evidence to convict them, or anyone for that matter, the town still muttered and whispered and kept their distance. Now Alex is gone and Farrah is simply known as, "that one spooky lady who only comes out in the day." Farrah doesn't go out at night. Not ever. She can't bare to look at the moon. She knows that every time she does, she can feel Tommy, looking right back at her. Looking with wild eyes and a furious rage. The spirit of Hemlock coursing through Tommy's veins, lashing out and trying sink it's hooks into Farrah's soul as well. She feels it without fail, every time she sees the moon.

51

What Crawls and Creeps

What can be done when there's no place to hide
From the bumps in the night and our darkness inside?
When we feel something crawling and creeping within
We must face the shadows slithering under our skin.

PARALYSIS

I'm trying to sleep
but I'm lying awake
I've nowhere to be
But I feel that I'm late
The pressure is mounting
I feel crushed from the weight
I know that it's nothing
But I still feel afraid
I just want to sleep
Still wide awake

I cannot get comfortable
Tossing and turning
The door wasn't locked
The creatures are stirring
Something from under my bed is emerging
Now I'm frozen in place,
And something is lurking

Closer and closer
The floorboards are creaking
The walls are all moving
The shadows are creeping
I can't make a sound
inside I'm screaming
Closer and closer
It's coming
it sees me.

Closer still
It's on top of me now
It leans in for the kill
It's cloaked in a shroud
It pulls back the veil
It unhinges its mouth
And...

AAAHHHHHHHHHHHHHHHHHHH!!!!!!!!

Hands to Yourself

Emily looked up at her mother as she tucked her into bed.
"Goodnight Mommy." she said softly as she turned over
on her side.

"Sweet dreams." Her mother replied as she kissed her on
the forehead.

Emily squirmed a bit under the covers, trying to get
comfortable. The blanket was stuck underneath Emily, she
flailed her right arm almost hitting her mother, and grunted as
she tugged at the stubborn sheet.

"Shh, shh… calm down baby. I got you" her mom shushed
as she helped her pull the blanket out from beneath her and
smoothed it down gently. "Keep those hands to yourself silly,
and sleep nice and tight." She kissed her cheek and turned to
exit the room.

"But my hand is under the bed." Emily replied abruptly.

Emily's mother stopped in her tracks and looked back at
her daughter, "Sorry?"

"That hand, it's under my bed." Emily repeated, sleepily.

"Silly girl," she laughed as she stepped back towards the
edge of Emily's bed. "Both your arms and hands are right
there on your sides."

"Well then whose arm is that?"

Emily was looking down out the side of her eyes, her
mother followed her gaze to the floor where she was staring at
one long, pale, white arm sticking out from under the bed.

The hand waved. As if to say hello. Emily's mother's jaw
dropped. The hand reached out before she had time to think. It

grabbed her by the ankle and pulled her down into the screaming darkness.

"Sweet dreams," whispered Emily as she smiled and drifted off to sleep.

The Curious Case of the Face On The Wall

By the time Kellen pulled into the driveway of his townhome on Leonard Ave, it had already gotten dark. Practice had gone later than usual and he was exhausted. He marched into the house and dropped his equipment bag by the door. He walked to the kitchen in zombie-like fashion, following the same routine he always did; Glass of water-crushed ice, filled to the top. Down the water. Grab an orange. (he'd peel it later.)

Kellen left the orange on the counter next to his keys. He couldn't believe how tired he was. Then it was down the hall to his bedroom, he started to take his jersey off as he walked. A long shower was in order and it was going to feel glorious. As he got to his room, he threw his jersey into his hamper from the doorway and reached around the wall to flick on the lights, without even looking. But when he reached around to hit the lights, same as he always did, he was confounded to feel something… different. It was not the plain plastic rectangular plate with a toggle switch in the middle that he flicked on and off every day. Instead, where the switch should have been, there was something soft and… fleshy. Surely, he was just tired, maybe his gel or pomade or some weird sort of substance had been flung on the wall when he got ready this morning, he had been in a rush after all. He moved his hand down to try and find the switch that should have been there, same as it always was. But when he moved his hand, he only felt more of this, this thing. It was round and partly smooth, partly a little rough and stubbly feeling… like… like a face. He had to be tired out of his mind. At this point the logical conclusion would have been to step into the room and simply look at the wall, where the switch was supposed to be, but Kellen was so put off by the strangeness of what was occurring that he couldn't move his feet. He stayed in the doorway and continued to move his hand over this disgusting… thing. He moved his fingers a bit to the left and now he was sure, absolutely sure that he felt a protruding nose. It was like half of a nose, which was absolutely insane but he was sure that he felt what had to be half of a face sticking out of his wall where the light switch should be. No. It couldn't be. "I'm just tired," he thought. He sighed out loud and muttered under his breath, "What in the-"

That's when he felt it move, under his fingers what was most likely the cheek of this bizarre face he was feeling *moved*. It rose to the side as if the face broke out in a wide smile. Then he felt a sharp breath come out the side of its mouth. He quickly pulled his hand away. His head was swimming. He was disgusted, appalled, terrified, enraged. None of this made any sense. He was entirely too exhausted to deal with any of this. He took a deep breath, pulled the phone from his pocket, turned on the flashlight app and jumped around the corner of his bedroom doorway.

"Ok! Who are you!?" He shouted, as he held out the light from his phone, in the most threatening and least comical way he could manage. But when the light shone on the wall, right where his hand had just been, right where the switch should have been, where he ran his fingers across that disturbing fleshy face… there was the light switch. The same plastic rectangular plate with a toggle switch in the middle that was always there. No face. Nothing out of the ordinary.

"Bro. What? "Kellen laughed to himself, "I need to get my head checked. What in the world…" he trailed off as he flicked on the lights in his room.

Still, he knew what he felt. That thing moved; you can't just imagine that. Can you? He felt slightly relieved but was still on edge. What if it just moved somewhere else in the house? Was it going to pop up somewhere else? Around another corner? He searched the walls of his room, nothing. Opened the closet slowly and cautiously, moved through each of his articles of hanging clothing, nothing. Under the bed, in the attached bathroom, nothing. It had to be in his head. Maybe he should start taking it easier at practice. He decided he would call his doctor in the morning. Just in case. He had read a lot about sports injuries; he knew they were not something to joke about. What he didn't know was what in the world he had just experienced.

He couldn't shake the feeling, no matter what he did his skin was still crawling. The shower didn't help, he was terrified to even grab the bottle of shampoo. Every corner he turned and every surface he touched, all he could think about was where the face would pop up next. He never wanted to feel this way again. He went back to the kitchen to grab the orange he had laid out when he got home, but when he saw the porous skin of the fruit, he just couldn't do it. He shivered and turned off the lights to the kitchen. Then the living room lights, and the hallway.

"I'll sleep it off," he said to himself, "sleep, and forget about... ALL of this in the morning."

He closed his bedroom door. His hand floated in the air and paused for a timid second before switching off the lights. He laughed to himself as he got into bed, "crazy..." he muttered. He lay down on his stomach. His head hit his wonderfully fluffy and comfortable pillow and he started to forget. His eyes were heavy. He was incredibly tired. He reached his hands under his pillow like he always did, and just as he was about to fall into the deepest sleep of his life, he felt... something.

There was a hole in his mattress, right under his pillow. That hole was NOT there this morning. Furthermore, it wasn't just a hole it was... wet? He moved his fingers. The sides of the hole were moist and rubbery, almost like- Like a mouth. Then he felt hard, jagged little bones. It was teeth. It was a mouth. There was a human mouth... In his mattress. Under his pillow.

"No!" he said out loud as his eyes shot open, but before he could pull his fingers away there was a loud CRUNCH, and a SNAP and Kellen screamed and screamed and screamed...

The Inky Black

Mom says, never leave the basement door open. She never says why or gives a reason. She just gets really, really mad if we don't keep that thing shut. My older brother Jason says it's because there's all types of bugs and creepy crawlies down there and Mom doesn't want 'em getting into the house. I think he just wants to scare me. Dad says, don't even go down there, he doesn't want us messing with his tools he says. Sometimes though, sometimes I open the door, and I stand at the top of the stairs and look down into the inky black darkness. You can't even see down past the seventh step, it's so dark in there. You can't even turn the lights on 'cause the rope for the light is hanging somewhere down by the twelfth step. Sometimes if I stare long enough my eyes start to play tricks on me, and it looks like the darkness is moving and pulsing like my heartbeat, sometimes I see dark black slithery, little tentacles reaching up out of the black but, I know that's in my head because well, Mom said so.

Yesterday morning I was walking to the kitchen, to get myself some cereal before my favorite cartoon started, you know the one with all the ninjas and the giant robots? I love that show. So, I'm walking down the hall and as I passed the basement door, I swear that I heard a noise coming from behind it. It kind of sounded like a crash so I thought maybe my dad was down there working with his tools or something, but now that I think about it, that wouldn't make any sense because Mom says Dad was at work yesterday morning but at the time, I didn't really think it through. So, I opened the door and I called out for my Dad and I waited for a pretty long time and as I was standing there, I was staring into that deep pit of darkness again. After a little while I swear, I saw it move up one of the steps. Like, the darkness was kind of like expanding, I guess? I don't know but it made my skin feel hot and itchy, like when Mom makes me wear that scratchy wool sweater. So, I'm standing there kind of frozen and I don't hear my Dad call back so I was about to turn around and close the door but all of a sudden Jason's favorite baseball comes rolling along the floor and bounces right over my feet and fell into the basement! For a second everything felt like it was in slow motion. I watched it fall and slowly bounce down each step until it rolled to a stop *right-on-**the 6th step**!* Remember I said how the lights disappears at the 7th step? Ok this probably sounds crazy but *for real*, it looked like it was resting on the edge of the shadowy darkness down there.

I think I was frozen for a long time looking at that baseball, because I think I heard the beginning of my favorite cartoon coming from the tv in the distance and I know that I had made time for cereal *before* the show was supposed to start. (Mom says I pay way too much attention to my "silly shows" and she says "If you only paid that much attention in school." You know, stuff all moms say) So, I'm standing there watching the ball when I hear this *THUMP* *THUMP* *THUMP* coming up behind me. It was Jason, chasing after his precious ball and blowing steam out of his ears.

"Why is the door open Twerp!?" he says to me. Like it's my fault that he was playing ball in the house even though Dad *always* tells him not to. He says that and he pushes me to the side and looks at where the thing landed, right there on the 6th step, and you know what he said next?

"Well, go on and get it."

He actually told *me* to get *his* ball! So, I whirl around and I say, "*What!?* Get it yourself Jason!"

"No way," he says, "you're the dweeb who opened the basement door and let my ball roll right past your big clumsy, clown shoes and down the stairs! Now go down there and get my ball or else I'll tell Dad that you were down there messing with his tools!"

Now, normally, I wouldn't take that kind of bullying but you know… he's my older, bigger, stronger brother… what am I gonna do? And I did *not* want him telling on me to Dad, even if it was all lies. Dad's the type to punish first and get the full story later. So, I shrugged my shoulders, I turned around and took the deepest breath possible. I kept trying to tell myself, "I can do this. No big deal. It's only on the 6th step, at least I can see the thing, right? Easy peezy." but all I could see was the deep inky black oozing out right underneath the ball, creeping up the walls and onto the next step. I take another breath but my jerk of a brother interrupts my concentration.

"Hurry up dork! I'm waiting."

I took one step down, not so bad, the step was sturdy, I could still see and the ball was just that much closer. I thought to myself, "Maybe it's not so scary." I took another step and the creaking noise that the second stair let out had to be the loudest most gut-wrenching thing I ever heard in my life. It sounded like the wood was stretching the walls in the house apart, it made my skull want to split open. I guess I flinched when that happened because I heard Jason laugh and call me a baby under his breath. It made me angry but it also gave me a little more fire in my chest to keep going. That's what Dad always calls it, fire in your chest. So, I get down to the third step and then the fourth, I was so close I could almost reach the ball from there but still not quite close enough so I took one more step down. There I was, one foot on the fifth step, one foot on the fourth and just in arms reach of my brother's oh-so-special baseball. I crouched down to grab the thing and that's when I heard the scariest blood curdling thing that I've ever heard.

"Daaaaaaaaaaavvvvviiiiiiidddddddddd…"

Something down there whispered my name! I completely froze with my hand right above Jason's baseball. I stared into the darkness and I watched it, I couldn't look away from it. It felt like I was in a staring competition with nothingness. Then it started moving, or maybe it was just my eyes getting watery but for real, it looked like the darkness was bubbling and wiggling around and folding over itself and crawling out of its massive black emptiness, and it was coming up the stairs. Then I heard it whisper something else, but it was so low and far away that I couldn't make out the words. I tried to listen harder but again my impatient brother interrupted.

"Dave!"

He caught me off guard and made my heart leap out of my chest. I scooped up the ball and jumped about 2 feet in the air, stumbling a bit when I landed which almost made me tumble backwards into that terrible abyss. I turned and ran up the last three steps probably faster than my little legs have ever gone before. I hurtled through the doorway and shoved the ball into my brother's hands so hard that he took a couple steps backwards.

"Woah! Scaredy cat, calm down!" he huffed as I ran past him crying all the way to the kitchen.

Look, I don't normally admit to crying but that was very-scary- stuff. My brother bounced his ball in his hand and said something as he walked away, he says that he told me to "shut the door next time" but I didn't hear him, I didn't hear anything but static for a good 5 minutes after all that. I leaned against the cabinets and just tried to catch my own breath. When I finally calmed down, I made myself a bowl of cereal and went to watch my cartoons before they ended.

After all that, after a few hours of Saturday morning cartoons and successfully forgetting about all things dark and scary, Mom got us all ready and took us to the market. It was a pretty normal Saturday afternoon, we got everything we needed and Mom even let me grab a couple of comic books from the news stand on the way out, everything was good, until we came home.

When we got back to the house, there wasn't really any house left, just a few wooden floorboards and a couple of roof shingles that we watched get swallowed up by a giant black hole in the ground. The hole was the deepest darkest thing you ever saw, with black energy floating around it and huge black tentacles slithering out of it. The tentacles were grabbing any pieces of the house that they could, pulling them back down into that pit that looked like a starless midnight sky flipped upside down and sucked into the earth.

We all sat in the car watching everything we owned disappear into the dark. I can't tell what that felt like but my mom says it's called "dread." I felt a whole lot of dread right then. I mean it was all gone and all my fault, if Jason could have just shut the door for me! Ugh, it didn't matter, the house was gone and that darkness was coming for us next. I watched as one of the slithery, slimy, black tentacles wiggled its way towards Mom's van. I watched her hands turn red as she gripped the steering wheel so hard, I thought she might rip it off. She turned her head slowly and looked at me and Jason, her eyes were black, she opened her mouth slowly and screamed in a deep booming voice;

"WHICH ONE OF YOU LEFT THE BASEMENT DOOR OPEN!?!?"

Jason and I both pointed at each other at the same time. He looked at me and his eyes were all black too, he says so were mine but I couldn't tell, and before either of us could let out a, "No, You!" that giant black tentacle wrapped itself around Mom's van and pulled us all down into that bubbling black hole… if only we had shut that basement door.

Midnight Snack

At the stroke of midnight, Terri was awoken by her own rumbling stomach. She opened her eyes. Her room was dark and quiet, the only lights were the glowing green stars stuck to her ceiling and the soft, red radiance of the large number twelve followed by a semicolon and two zeros on her digital alarm clock.

"Uggghhhh.." she groaned, annoyed of being stirred from her precious slumber. She rolled over and tried to fall back asleep but her stomach rumbled again, it even gurgled a bit this time.

"Fiiiiiine!" she mumbled angrily.

Terri let one leg drop off the side of the mattress, followed slowly by the other, and she pulled herself off the bed. She rose like a zombie and dragged her feet across the bedroom floor, her eyes were barely open. As she reached the door to her bedroom she reached out to the hallway and fumbled for the light switch right outside her room. The lights flickered on and she had to stop and rub her eyes. Her stomach let out another short growl.

"Oh, shut up," she whispered, "I'm going, I'm going."

Plodding down the hallway, Terri pulled the sleeves of her pajama shirt over her hands and wrapped both arms around her stomach. She made her way slowly to the kitchen, turned on another light and opened the door to her refrigerator. Her stomach let out a tiny gurgle as the refrigerator light crawled its away across Terrie's face and spilled onto the kitchen floor. She had to squint her eyes as they adjusted.

"Ok…" she said quietly to herself as she rummaged through the contents of the fridge.

She moved a container of vanilla yogurt to the side, "No…"

She picked up an old sandwich wrapped in cellophane, "hmm..." she brought it closer to her face and took a sniff, "Nope. Definitely no." Terri lobbed the stinky sandwich back on the shelf, too tired to throw it away. Her stomach groaned, it almost sounded like it was crying.

She moved a large container of purple liquid to the side, "There you are." Terri reached behind the juice bottle and pulled out a large rectangular plastic container. She held the container up to the light and examined the contents, the beveled sides of the plastic tub made it hard to see but she could still make out a large red mound of some sort of glistening, slimy meat. Terri licked her lips, closed the refrigerator door and shuffled her way over to the kitchen table.

Terri's stomach let out one more bubbling, ferocious growl, she could feel it travel from her guts up to her throat. "Shh, shh, shh... Mommy's got our midnight snack riiight here." she hummed as she rubbed her belly. Terri stood by the edge of the table and popped open the lid, the pungent aroma of sour ammonia immediately wafted out of the tub. Terri looked down at the pile of bloody, rotten meat in her container and rubbed her stomach again.

"Ok. Do your thing," she began to lift the bottom of her sleep shirt just over her navel, "make it quick though yeah? I'm tired."

As she rolled up her shirt, a thin line stretched across her waist. The line got deeper and darker and then suddenly her stomach split open, revealing long thin lips that stretched from one hip to the next. Inside the new mouth on Terri's torso were a few sharp pointy teeth and one giant pink tongue. The mouth began to pant and twitch its lips excitedly. The tongue extended itself and reached out across the table and into the container of rancid meat. The tongue wrapped itself around the meat and pulled the entire stinking mass into its mouth. Terri's second mouth closed and began to chew loudly and sloppily. It smacked its lips together and gnashed its pointy teeth, as it masticated its meal, grunting and snarling.

"Ugh. Do you have to be such a slob?" Terri asked, annoyed as she watched herself eat.

The mouth on her stomach chewed a bit more and then swallowed the rest in one large gulp. The mouth then licked its teeth, panting happily.

"Good," she said as she patted her midriff above the monstrous cavity in her gut, "Now no more crying or misbehaving. Momma needs her sleep."

The mouth licked its lips one last time with its long twisty tongue and seemed to smile as it slid away, disappearing once again inside of Terri's stomach. Terri rolled down her shirt, turned off all the lights and waddled back to her bed, exhausted and full.

The Nightmare Above

It was a quiet Wednesday night in Marie and Anthony's spacious yet modest two-bedroom apartment. The first quiet night that Marie and Anthony had experienced in about 9 months. They had just put their 9-month-old daughter to sleep via an almost suspiciously successful bedtime routine. No tears, no wailing, their daughter Anette had gone to sleep without a fight for the first time that they could remember and they were not about to question it. The couple closed the child's bedroom door as cautiously as possible and crept down the hallway where they turned to each other both brimming with smiles and gave a very silent high-five. They moved to the living room and turned on their video baby monitor.

"Awe," said Marie, "she looks so sweet when she's sleeping."

Anthony looked over Marie's shoulder, "Is she smiling?" he asked.

"Oh my gosh, I think she is! Our little angel."

Marie rested her head on Anthony's shoulder and Anthony rested his head on top of hers and they both cuddled for a moment just watching their little girl, admiring her innocence and relishing in their new found peace and quiet. After a few more blissful minutes, Anthony checked his watch.

"Wow. It's only 8:30 babe, we have never had this much time to kill!"

"What do we do?" Marie asked excitedly.

"Let's watch a movie," said Anthony reaching for the television remote, "when is the last time we got to watch a full movie in its entirety?"

"A scary movie?" asked Marie looking up at her husband with wide eyes and a smile.

"Oh yes." he answered as he began to scroll through the available movies on their cable subscription.

After a lot of scrolling and mild debate (Anthony wanted to watch an older classic horror film but Marie didn't want anything too cheesy, and they both agreed absolutely no scary movies that involved children) they finally settled on a Werewolf movie that had particularly good acting and what they both thought was an exceptionally well written script.

10 minutes into the movie and they were both fast asleep on the couch. In all their excitement they had forgotten to account for the immeasurable amount of exhaustion that comes with raising a child. They slept for a good 30 minutes before they were awakened by a loud bang. The couple jumped off the couch in a dazed panic and they both shouted simultaneously.

"Anette!?"

Marie quickly swiped the video monitor off of the coffee table before Anthony could even reach for it. They looked at the screen together, expecting to see Anette throwing stuffed animals or pillows and screaming or worse, Anette out of the crib somehow. The video monitor however, still showed one happily sleeping baby, completely undisturbed. Marie collapsed on the couch and ran her hand through her hair as she let out a loud sigh of relief.

"Oh, I thought that was going to be so bad," she said.

"Yeah but you definitely heard *something* right?" asked Anthony as he scanned the rest of the apartment, searching for the source of the sound that had stirred his slumber.

"I mean I think I did, it could have been a dream…"

"A dream that we both had and both woke up from at the same time?" he asked incredulously.

"...or the movie?"

"No way, that was way too loud. I felt it in my chest."

They both paused as they looked around the apartment, Marie muted the movie and they waited in silence, both trying to play detective in their own heads. Then they heard it again. This time it was even louder and more intense.

BANG BANG BANG

They both looked up at the ceiling. It was coming from above. Their apartment was on the first floor of a five-story complex, it must have been coming from the tenants in the apartment directly above them.

"What the heck are they doing up there?" Anthony demanded.

"I swear if they wake her up..."

"Check the monitor-"

"She's fine." Marie cut him off, she had checked the monitor as soon as the banging started again, "wasn't even phased by it somehow."

"Man, she must have been exhausted. She never sleeps this heavy," said Anthony as he plopped down on the couch next to his wife, "They better knock it off though," he looked up again, and then looked at his watch, "sounds like they're trying to play basketball indoors at 9 o'clock at night."

"On a Wednesday," added Marie.

"Right? If they keep it up, I'm going to have to go up there."

"Just call the complex security, that's what they're there for." said Marie as she yawned and leaned her head backwards into the couch.

"I don't think you're allowed to make a noise complaint until after 10 pm." Anthony replied grabbing the remote and unmuting the movie, "Do you want to restart it? I fell asleep like right at the beginning."

Marie laughed, "Yeah, me too. I'll make us coffee," she got up and walked to the kitchen area while Anthony was rewinding the film.

They made their coffee, restarted the movie and snuggled into each other once more getting as cozy as possible. The noise had seemingly ceased and they were both just awake enough to thoroughly enjoy their movie in an almost dreamlike state. They made it all the way to the third act, right around the part where the father reveals that he is also a werewolf and a thrilling battle ensues, before the two started to nod off again. But just as the action ramped up and just as Anthony let out one single snore, there was another *BANG* from above. This one so loud that it shook the walls of the apartment.

Marie jumped off the couch and swooped up the baby monitor in one motion as she started down the hall towards Anette's room. She was still in a stupor but she was sure that whatever that was it must have startled her daughter awake, as it had her and her husband. Anthony let out a snort as he jumped off the couch, he brushed his long hair out of his face and tried to wipe the sleep off his face with both hands.

As he came to, he shouted, "What the-"

BANG! BANG! BOOM!

"Marie!? Where's Anette!?" he shouted down the hall over the incessant banging.

"She's... she's fine," Marie's voice came from halfway down the hall. She had stopped to look at the monitor and saw that their little girl was as blissful as ever, she had moved her hand once over her tiny little blanket, but her eyes stayed shut and her face was still serene. Anthony came bounding down the hall to his wife's side.

"Are you sure," he asked as he reached for the monitor. He had to see for himself, "How?" he said in disbelief.

"Maybe terrible loud noises are the trick?" guessed Marie half joking as she threw her hands in the air.

The banging started again; it was coming from directly above their living room. It was no longer just banging either, now it sounded as if something was being dragged across the floor above them violently from side to side, followed by more banging and what sounded like an immensely large person sprinting back and forth.

"Nope," Anthony paced the living area as he pulled out his phone and dialed the number for security, "Absolutely not, this is not ok!"

"What is wrong with these people!?" Marie seethed through her teeth as she looked at the ceiling half expecting the tenants above her to notice her rage filled gaze piercing through their floor.

Anthony finished talking to the security guard and tossed his phone on the couch. The banging had not yet stopped.

"He said he's on his way up there, is she still sleeping?" Anthony talked as calmly as his temper would allow over the calamity coming from upstairs.

"She's ok, but there's no way she's going to stay asleep if they don't STOP THIS!" she shouted the last two words into the empty space above their heads. It was too much, she couldn't take it and she couldn't wait for the security guard to take his sweet time. Marie grabbed the broom out of the closet and jumped onto the couch.

"Marie wait," Anthony started but Marie was not listening. Marie was in Mama Bear mode and Mama Bear was pissed. She slammed the butt of the broomstick against the ceiling three times as hard as she could.

BOOM BOOM BOOM!

She stood there staring up and breathing vehemently, she had some choice words she wanted to scream at them but she decided more yelling wasn't going to help their situation so she held her tongue.

The banging stopped. The credits were rolling on the movie.

"Well," said Marie stepping down from the couch and returning the broom to the closet, "Hopefully, that is that, for the night." she walked over to Anthony, hugged him and put her face into his chest and muttered, "I'm so tired."

"Me too babe." Anthony ran his hand through her hair and kissed the top of her head.

Knock! Knock! Knock!

They both jumped at the same time, their hearts pounding. This time the noise was not from above however, it was the front door of their apartment.

"Security guard." they said it at the same time as they smiled at each other.

Anthony opened the door to a very short and stocky man in a puffy black jacket with a shiny plastic security badge fastened to the lapel that bore the guards name: G E R R Y. Gerry was also wielding a large black flashlight in his right hand.

Gerry coughed and hacked a little bit before he spoke, "Yous guys 108? You made the call about the uh, disturbance from apartment 208?"

Anthony looked at the large numbers on his door that clearly said 108. "Um. Yes sir, I made the call. Those guys have been going at it all night and we have a 9-month-old child trying to sleep down here, and it was really out of control. Where they bowling up there or what?" Asked Anthony with a nervous laugh.

"Well," started Gerry adjusting the leather glove on his left hand, "well that *guy, singular,* that guy up in 208... he says he wasn't making no noise and in fact when I was up there having a very polite conversation, what I heard was a banging coming from his floor as if maybe someone in *your* domicile had perhaps used a broom or uh, maybe a mop, with which to hit your ceiling and bother your upstairs neighbor."

"Woah, woah, what!?" started Marie as she joined Anthony's side. "There is no way that's possible! Someone was up there stomping around like a herd of elephants!"

"Are you sure you went to the right apartment?" asked Anthony.

Gerry the security guard shined his light at the number on their door, "One, oh, eight."
Then he shined the light upwards towards the hallway ceiling and said "Two, oh, eight."
He clicked off his flashlight and shrugged at the couple, "I've done all I can do folks, I told him that even though I don't believe it was him, I told him to make sure to keep it down anyways. Now I'm sorry but there ain't much else I can do or say and, from the sound of it," he poked his head inside the apartment and turned his ear to listen, "Seems like whatever it was you was hearing has stopped don't it? You folks have a good night, now." Gerry turned and walked down the complex hallway whistling to himself quietly.

Marie was at a loss for words. Anthony blew the hair out of his eyes and put his hands on his hips.

"Well… at least it's stopped."

"I hope so. I'd really rather not deal with them or *Gerry* again."

"Bed?"

"Please."

The couple turned and shut the door to their apartment. They made their way to the bedroom, they checked the monitor one more time, Anette was still sound asleep.

"I think I want to go in there," said Marie as she looked down at the screen, "I know she's ok, but I just need to feel her breathing and blow her a kiss."

She could tell by Anthony's face that he didn't think it was a good idea.

"I will be like a ninja I swear!"

Anthony smiled as he lifted the sheets, "Just go, you're fine. If she slept through all of that, there's no way you'll wake her up."

"Right?" Marie laughed and exited the room.

Anthony grabbed the monitor and sat down in bed, he watched as Marie slowly crept into Anette's room and stood over her crib. Marie gently placed a hand on Anette's chest and then quickly took it away. Marie, who had a feeling that Anthony was watching, turned to the camera and gave a thumbs up. Anthony smiled and placed the monitor on his night stand, then slid down into a comfortable position under the covers, shut his eyes, and let himself start to drift as he waited for Marie to return to bed. All was calm and peaceful, Anthony had just about fell asleep when suddenly, the banging started again. Just one loud knock at first, quickly followed by seven more rapid and powerful knocks from the roof above their living room.

"Are you kidding me!?" Anthony shouted as he jumped out of the bed. He shoved his feet into his shoes and threw on a jacket as he stormed out of the bedroom and tore through the living room muttering to himself, "...should of taken care of this myself," he threw open the door and yelled over his shoulder, "Be right back!" as he left the apartment, shut the door and marched towards the complex stairs leading up to apartment 208.

He arrived at the door of his upstairs neighbor and pounded on it with all the fury of an entire SWAT team. The door handle started to turn and Anthony clenched his fists, his palms were sweaty and his heart was beating fast.

The door swung open and standing inside was a tall man with pale skin short blonde hair and very thin lips. The man was wearing a white apron over a stained white t-shirt and dirty blue jeans. To Anthony's horror, the man's apron was covered in crimson red hand prints, splatters and smudges. The man looked shifty and irritated, his hands were also dirty and covered in black and red smudges and they were nervously ringing out an even dirtier cloth rag.

"Can I help you?" the man asked. His tone was rushed and shaky but he also sounded quite annoyed.

Anthony put his hands on his hips, "Uh, yeah! You can help me by knocking off whatever you're tryin' to pull up here man! I got a baby down there that's trying to sleep and-"

Anthony stopped himself short as he eyed his neighbor up and down, he stared at the red markings on his apron for a moment.

"Look, I don't know what you're up to but… If I have to get the cops involved I will." he said sternly.

"Cops?" the tall man's face dropped, "for what reason? I think you may have the wrong apartment. Honestly." he pleaded with his eyes.

Anthony pointed at the numbers on the door, "208?" then he pointed at his own chest, "108."

"Ok."

"Yeah." Anthony raised his eyebrows aggressively.

"Ok," the man stepped to the side and stretched out his arm towards his living room," I can show you exactly what I've been up to and maybe we can resolve this, civilly. Would you like to come in?"

Anthony wasn't sure how he felt about the idea, the man's posture was imposing but his demeanor was meek and vulnerable. The read smears on his apron made Anthony more uncomfortable than anything but his curiosity was still getting the better of him, he was dying to know what could have possibly made such calamitous noise, especially if this man was alone. In a slightly fugue state, Anthony shrugged his shoulders and stepped into the man's house.

"My name is William by the way. Will is fine, and you?"

"Anthony," he grunted looking around the apartment for any clues to what could have caused so much ruckus. He found nothing. The place was calm and quiet, dimly lit. Will's furniture was mostly deep burgundy and charcoal, he had three candles lit on a coffee table. There was an aroma of cloves and cinnamon in the air, and something else, like the spices were trying to mask the stench of something acrid. Anthony traced the area on the floor above his own living room, looking for any signs of commotion but all he found was a grey carpet beneath a black coffee table. "Impossible," he thought to himself. He kept his eyes on the floor and as he followed the trail to where the tv in his own apartment would be, his eyes stumbled upon the edges of a bunched up white sheet, flecked with more red splatters. His heart beat faster. He kept looking, the white sheet was covered in red, the rest of it sprawled beneath three wooden legs of what? Some sort of torture device? No. Anthony's tired eyes ran up the wooden legs and he had to laugh to himself when he realized what he was looking at. It was an easel, an easel with a fresh canvas displaying William's newest painting, a still life portrait of a bowl of red apples, the paint was still wet. It was actually quite good thought Anthony.

"As you can see," said Will as he walked up slowly behind Anthony, "My 'wild and crazy nights' consist mostly of paint and incense and old jazz records. I'm not a classically trained artist, my work is rather drab, but I do love it." he sighed.

"No, no, it's uh, it's great... I can't do that, I mean," Anthony fumbled his words as he scratched his head and fussed with his hair, "I just, I guess you're not what- er, this-" he put out his arms, "*this*, is just not what I expected. I thought I was going to have to come up here and fight somebody" he rubbed his eyes. He felt foolish, and tired out of his mind.

"Oh lord," laughed Will, "I couldn't hurt a-"

BOOM BOOM BOOM

The noise came from the floor beneath them, Anthony could feel it shake the bones in his shins. He cocked his head to the side and looked at Will with wild eyes. Will threw his hands up in front of himself and shook his head to signal, "that didn't come from me."

"Marie!" Anthony said out loud before sprinting for Will's door.

"Uh, nice meeting you!?" Will called after Anthony as he fled the apartment but Anthony didn't hear anything. All Anthony could hear was his own heartbeat filling his ears as he stomped down the stairwell and shot himself down the hall to his own apartment as fast as he could possibly go. He got to the door of 108 and grabbed the handle, he took two deep gasping breaths and flung the door open, what Anthony saw next he could have never prepared himself for. There, in the center of his living room, hanging upside down from the ceiling was some sort of monstrous demon. It was larger than Anthony, it's skin was a murky grey with wild patches of shaggy fur all over, it had the body of a man but the head of a wolf and giant black bat wings that were folded on its back, it's eyes were neon yellow with glowing red in the center. The entire thing was shaking violently and breathing like a rabid dog. The beast locked eyes with Anthony and stretched out his wings slowly, swiveled its own head around like an owl, and let out a bellowing roar. It was so loud and startling that it knocked Anthony backwards, falling to the floor on his rear. The creature then began to crawl across the ceiling rapidly, back in forth in every direction, all the while shaking its head and gnashing its jaws.

Anthony sat in shock, in a state of disbelief, his head was swirling so bad that he felt sick. He had to shake it off, he had to get his girls. He jumped to his feet and yelled for Marie down the hall. There was no answer from his wife but the demon on the ceiling stopped and started to turn slowly towards Anthony. He screamed for Marie again, still standing in the doorway. He was worried that if he ran to Anette's room, he would just be leading the monster directly to his girls. Had the beast already gotten to them? He had to take his chances, Anthony crouched into a running position and got ready to make a mad dash to the room when he suddenly felt a small hand on his shoulder.

"We're right here my love."

"Marie!" Anthony whipped himself around to find his beautiful wife, fully intact and out of harm's way, standing at the short end of the hallway, holding Anette in her arms. Anthony grabbed her and hugged them both intensely.

"I thought you were gone. We have to get out of here. We have to go now babe, ok? We need to get to the car and just-just…" Anthony pulled back from his wife and took a second to register her sudden change of outfit and the calm, almost serene look on her face, "Um. Babe? W-why are you wearing a robe and- and why is Anette's face covered by that- is that a veil? What-"

Anthony reached out to try and remove the black veil that was covering his daughter but Marie stepped back out of his grasp.

"We don't want to wake her darling. She's going to need all the rest she can get tonight."

Anthony put both hands on the sides of his head, "This can't be real. This is a dream. You're not making any sense, and that thing, *that thing!*" Anthony pointed into the apartment and looked inside, the creature was now perched on the arm of their living room couch, staring directly at Anthony, "Babe we have to go!!" he screamed and pleaded, his voice cracked as tears began to stream down his cheeks.

"We can't leave now dear," Marie said calmly as she held Anette in her right arm and pulled a tall pointy black hood over her head with her left, "Our guests are just starting to arrive."

"*Guests?*"

Anthony heard the shuffling of feet behind him, he turned around slowly and felt his blood run cold. The hallway was now filled with two long rows of figures in black cloaks with tall pointy hoods filing their way down the hall towards him.

Anthony turned back to Marie, "Look, I don't know what this is but just- just let me have Anette and we'll leave and let you do whatever, *this* is."

"This, my dear, is a blood ritual, a sacrifice."

Anthony's fear started to turn to anger.

"You will *not* sacrifice my daughter!"

"Of course not, my love," said Marie with a smile as two hands clamped down on each of Anthony's shoulders, "Tonight's sacrifice is You."

Anthony tried to protest but a third hand wrapped around his mouth. The cloaked figures overpowered poor Anthony and dragged him kicking and squirming into apartment 108, making sure to shut the door behind them. And the night finally became quiet once again.

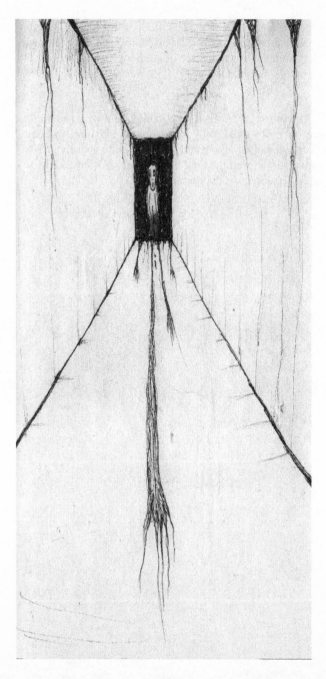

WHAT LIES IN THE DEEP

From prophetic visions through cryptic transmissions
We peer into our deepest and darkest premonitions.
What lies in that ghostly, foreboding abyss?
What waits in the end? Was it all just a glitch?

DEEP BELOW, DEEP WITHIN

Between the walls
Beneath the skin
There's something crawling
Deep within.
Up in the attic
Under the floors
something is clawing
it's way to the doors
deep down in the dark
deeper down than we go
beneath the abyss
deeper down than we know
something is coming
some terrible thing
something far worse
than the worst of our dreams
you know this is true
because you've felt it too
what lies deep within?
is it inside of you?

Bubble Guts

Have you recently ingested any foods, or beverages containing Carbectomis? Have you been feeling symptoms of discomfort in your stomach and/or lower abdomen? If yes, then what are you doing? Stop reading this immediately and seek professional medical help!

Nasty stuff that Carbectomis. It's all over the place now, and you know what it does to you right? I would suggest you watch what you eat and if you ever feel your stomach rumbling, make sure you hold your breath and plug your nose for at least 45 seconds to ensure you suffocate what may or may not be currently swimming around your insides, and then, seek immediate medical attention, like I said.

Here, let me explain. Some time ago in the 21st century, some genius in a nice, freshly-pressed white lab coat in some fancy laboratory full of holographic computers and test tubes, with multi-functioning laser focused microscopes and all the bells and whistles, there they came up with what they thought at the time was a really great idea. What that genius invented was an entirely new microbial creature never before seen on the planet earth and they called it; Carbectomis! Carbectomis was revolutionary! Hailed by the Times and science journals alike as one of the greatest innovations in modern history. It was the end all-be all answer to the world's dietary needs. It was the diet without a diet, a little "Carbec" sprinkled on your food or in your drink and It would attack every carb and fat cell you had ingested *and* it would have a nice little feast on your preexisting fat cells. Not only would it do that, but it would clean up and clean out your guts on the way down with *seemingly* no side effects whatsoever! It was a work out with no work out. It was humanity's greatest gift to humanity.

It was a parasite is what it was, but we all took well over way too long to figure that out. What we didn't see, what we couldn't possibly have detected, was what those tiny little buggers were doing inside of us the whole time. We couldn't see it because it was on such a submicroscopic scale that our most advanced equipment couldn't pick it up. What those little freaks were doing, as they cleaned us out and gave us our perfect model beach bodies, after they feasted, they would lay tiny tiny almost atom-sized eggs in our stomachs. Those eggs would take years to grow and hatch but once they did, well, let's just say keeping your fit form was the least of your worries. What came out of those eggs, besides pure evil, were these football sized eel like creatures, mouth like a lamprey and hundreds of tiny little centipede arms... and that's just it's larval stage! If you're lucky, and I mean really lucky, you'll catch it then and you'll get it "taken care of." Thing is, the only symptom during that phase is a bad case of the bubble guts. What you feel is a little rumble in your tummy and let me tell you, that's no stomach gasses rumbling around in there... that is hundreds of tiny legs and muscles moving their way around inside of you! If you feel that, even the slightest hint, you seek help as fast as you possibly can because after that stage, if it grows any further, oh there's no stopping that little monster then.

The next stage is the pupal stage, where it grows skinny little spider arms with hooks and claws. Once it has those, it bursts through your intestines and crawls its way up the inside of your sternum, it grabs on to your lungs and sinks its teeth in. It uses your lungs like a gas mask. The pain is indescribable, you feel every little tear and cut that it makes as it traverses your innards and once it gets to those sweet air sacks, the burning that spreads through every one of your nerve endings will cripple you! After roughly 24 hours of excruciating, earth-shattering pain, you die and the parasite dies as well. But this is not the end for you or for them you see, as the two of your corpses rot together symbiotically... a fungus grows from inside of the parasite's husk of a body. This fungus grows and grows like veins made out of curdled milk, covering everything inside of you in webs of stinky, moldy fungus. Once that stuff is oozing out of your orifices like chalky mushrooms protruding from your eye sockets and ears and mouth, once it works its way up there, it crawls into your brain and takes over. Your body is suddenly reanimated as one of these "Shroomwalkers" fungus ridden zombies with giant stalks of fungus sticking out of their heads like ghostly antlers.

At that point, well, after that it's very easy to take care of you, or what's left of you. Those big guns in the army, they'll come in with their hazmat tanks, spray you down with fungicide, you go into shock, you convulse, you shrivel up and you die. I mean really die, for real this time.

And that's it. So, please be advised, whatever you do, be very very careful as to not take, ingest, or swallow anything that even remotely resembles Carbectomis. Please. For your sake and for ours. Thank you and be safe.

-Dr. Corvidchao

3:33AM

For the past two and a half, almost three weeks now, every night at exactly 3:33am I have been receiving very strange phone calls from a blocked phone number.

The first night was one of the most startling, but at that point I just assumed it was a wrong number. I picked up the phone half asleep, trying to look at the time on my wall projector but all I could make out was a glowing green blur. I answered the phone and before I could get out a sleepy "Hello?" I yanked the phone away from my ear. Coming through the speaker was what sounded like electronic screams drowning in ancient television static. It was loud, it felt abrasive, it shocked me wide awake. I tried to shout a confused "Hello?" over the static but it was still screaming at me. I hit the End button as many times as I could before it finally hung up. I slammed my phone back down on the nightstand, rolled over on my back, and said aloud, "Well that was terrible." I wondered about what exactly just happened for a good five minutes. Maybe someone's old dial-up internet had somehow misfired and dialed an actual phone number instead of connecting to the internet? Can that even happen? Does dial-up even exist anymore? It's not like I could call them back, the number was blocked. After a few more minutes of annoyed and exhausted confusion, my eyelids become heavy again and I fell back to sleep.

The second night, I slept through the call. Possibly from being so tired all day due to my lack of sleep from the previous night but that night I slept like a baby. Still, the same call came through at the same time and left a message very similar to what I heard when I answered my phone the night before. I tried listening to the message in the morning when I woke up, but it was just more electronic chaos. This time sounded as if there was metal scraping against metal in some sort of pattern but it was too loud and piercing to try and sit there and decipher anything from it. I deleted the message and went about my day. The fact that it happened at the same time further convinced me that perhaps this was some sort of malfunction from someone or something trying to access the internet at that certain time each night. Either way, I just hoped it was going to stop.

On the third night, I was annoyed. I had a very busy day to wake up to and this was beginning to ruin my sleeping patterns. I picked up my phone and in a bit of frustration and admittedly in a slightly childlike manor, I screamed back at my phone.

"Aaaggghhhblblblagghhh!! How do you like it!? People are trying to sleep you know!"

Then, for the first time, I heard silence. For whatever reason, that silence on the other end of the receiver was the most unsettling thing I had heard yet.

"H-h-hello?" I stammered, slightly sleepy and entirely creeped out. For a moment there was nothing. Then there was what sounded like a deep breath, a deep metallic breath… like a vacuum starting up and simultaneously pulling a long steel knife out of its sheath, it was bone chilling. Suddenly I was hit by the electronic screaming again. It felt like it had pierced my eardrum. My right ear was still ringing after I hung up. I hung up as fast as I could, a little bit out of frustration but mostly out of fear. That was too much. That shook something deep in my core. I kept hearing echoes of those terrible noises ringing in my head. I did not fall back asleep.

On the fourth, fifth, and sixth night… I turned off the vibration, put the ringer on silent and completely ignored my phone. I slept like a baby. That didn't stop the calls though. Each morning I woke up to a voice mail left at the same time, 3:33am. Each time left by the anonymous number and each time, I was greeted by a blood curdling cacophony of noise.

After a week of this harassment I decided to take my phone into the store where I bought it. The disheveled teenager working at the front desk informed me that all I had to do was go into my call settings and reject calls from blocked or private numbers. He also informed me that I could have easily looked all of this up on the internet myself and fixed my problem a long time ago. I did not appreciate his smug demeanor but I was grateful for his help. I followed his instructions and hoped that I was finally done with my phone stalker. I played him a few of the messages to see if he had any idea what they were all about or if anyone else had ever reported hearing something similar. He replied that while it was strange and "super creep status" he had never had anyone else report something like it. He also added that he had a friend who makes electronic music that would probably love to record a sample of the messages for one of his songs. I politely declined and left for home.

That night was the first night since this whole thing started that I did not receive any calls. Oddly enough I still woke up right around 3:33 and stared at my phone. It was like my body knew it was waiting for something, but nothing came. After a minute or two of radio silence, I fell asleep. It's finally over, I thought to myself. I dreamt that morning about being on an operating table and doctors and surgeons with black holes where their eyes should have been, replacing the blood veins in my body with electric wiring. I woke up in a cold sweat. It took me the rest of that day to shake off the nightmare. The only thing that helped me remove it from my mind was the thought of sleeping again and being free of those terrible phone calls. I could turn my ringer back on, I could enjoy my rest. That much at least I could look forward to.

Night number eight, 3:33am, my phone rang again. I almost didn't wake up but the buzzing against my nightstand wouldn't stop. In my dream-like state it almost sounded like my entire house was buzzing, I could feel it vibrating through my bed and in the walls and the floor. I shook it off and looked at my phone. I waited for the blurriness to clear up as I stared at my device, bewildered. This time there was a number. A number so strange I thought I might still be dreaming. The caller id showed: x146+113++00000. I don't know how long the trail of zeros went on for, the whole thing didn't even fit on my display. I also did not know that letters and symbols could be a part of a phone number. I was rattled but after everything, after all of this, I was starting to get more angry than scared. I had no way of telling that it was the same caller but something inside of me just knew. It was right on schedule, it was calling for me, and I was beyond ready to be done with them. I answered my phone.

"What do you want?" I huffed through gritted teeth.

They took a long pause but I could hear them, it was low but I could hear ragged breathing. Heavy wheezing breaths coming through some sort of ventilator. The breathing got louder and faster, suddenly a robotic voice shouted, "Y-y-y-you belong to R-r-render-r-r!"

Then the glitchy screaming turned into a sinister laugh. Sharp piercing laughter, wrought with buzzing electricity. It was as if each huffing breath of laughter was hitting the metal side on an old Operation board game. Every sound that the caller made I could feel in my skull. Each one traveled through my bones; I could feel the vibrations in my teeth. The laughter turned into more screaming and crunching and gnashing and buzzing. I began to get nauseous; my head was swimming and my own skin started to feel like a thick suit made of static. I slammed my phone down on the bed next to me and poked the end button over and over. I was sweating and my finger slipped on the screen, the noise was still blowing out my speakers. Finally, my finger and the button connected, the call ended and I sat there in my bed drenched in sweat and my ears still ringing. Why was this happening to me? Who or what is Render? I couldn't let them win, I had their number now, it was time to get some answers. I took a deep breath and tried to calm my nerves, it was no use, I was a ball of anxiety and delirium. My fingers were pins and needles. I took another quick breath, braced myself, and called the number back. It rang once, not even a full ring, it cut short and I was instantly greeted by an old "call cannot be completed as dialed" stock message. Of course. My hand dropped down and I held my phone by my side. I felt defeated. I could still faintly hear the autonomous voice repeating itself over and over.

"We're sorry. This call cannot be completed as dialed. Please hang up, and try your call again. - We're sorry. This call cannot be completed as dialed. Please hang up, and try your call again. -"

I let it go on, I rubbed my eyes until I was seeing stars. I was so out of it and drained I felt like I was floating in an endless void. Was this all just a dream? The phone kept talking in the background, like an ancient radio broadcast being transmitted across the vast emptiness of space...

"We're sorry. This call cannot be completed as dialed. Please hang up, and try your call again. - We're sorry. This call cannot be c-c-completed as d-d-die-dialed. Please hang up-HANG UP, and t-t-tr-tt-try.... We're sorry."

What was that? I didn't have the phone up to my ear but I could hear that the last message was definitely off. I picked it up again and listened, the voice sounded like it was much higher pitched now and it had been sped up. The machine was rattling off the message now twice as fast and it was starting to glitch. The cold, droning voice had turned into that of a crunchy, grimy gremlin spewing out a string of letters and static noise.

"We're ssss-S-s-Sorry. Thissss" more clanging and buzzing "cannot be c-c-complete- CAN. NOT" static "NOT COMPLETE. Nine. Seven. Nine. N-n-N-nine! Please hang up, please hang up, please hang up, HANG. UP."

"What is this?" I shouted over them, "What do you want from me!?"

Then the message stopped and for what felt like an eternity there was a low gravely static being emitted but nothing else. Then the static slowly started to rise. It rose to a point where it sounded like chains being dragged through a swarm of buzzing cicadas and right when it was almost too loud to bare, it spoke to me again. The voice that came through was sharp and piercing like a knife to the ears, it was covered in crackling electricity that made my hair stand on end. The line sizzled before it started to speak.

Szzzz..
   "YOU."
Szzz..*crackle*...bzzz
   "YOU."

It repeated again
"HAVE. BEEN. CHOSEN."

   More static.

"FOR. "..bzzz.." RENDING."

 Each word sounded like they had been typed into a text to speech computer program and then baked in a microwave. Then another more grim and sinister voice came through, this one sounded slightly more human but still robotic and empty.

"See you s-s-s-soon."
Click.
Click.
Dial tone....

Hearing that dial tone felt like getting a game over in an old arcade game where you had no option to return to a save point. The kind of dead end you feel in your chest. "Chosen for rending?" What does that even mean? Why me?

The only thing that I did know for sure, was that I wanted nothing to do with this anymore. Not a single thing. Not at all. I selected the number from my recent call list and elected to block it as quickly as I could. Still, it felt fruitless, deep down I knew that whoever or whatever was on the other end of that phone could still reach me if they wanted to and boy did it feel like they wanted to. I did not sleep that night either.

On the ninth night, or was it the tenth? (My days and nights have all started to blur together now.) Whichever night it was, I decided to simply turn off my phone before going to bed. After checking three to four times to make absolutely sure it was off. I finally got some well-deserved peace and quiet. Sure enough, the next morning once I turned on my phone, there was a new message from a new number. The number was similar to the last but only differentiated by a few numbers and characters. I couldn't bring myself to play the message. I couldn't stand to hear those awful noises or those terrifying voices one more time. At this point I was clearly being harassed and that last encounter surely felt like a threat, I decided to go to the police.

When I got to the station, I gave them my story, showed them the numbers that had called me and even played them the messages that I had not already deleted. The detective that I spoke to's first response was, "Now... You sure you're not just gettin' your wires crossed with say, a fax machine in perhaps another country? It could account for the strange number and the odd hours of the night at which they have been uh, contacting you."

He put his fingers up in air quotes when he said "contacting." I was beyond fed up but I tried to compose myself

"I'm sure." I replied sternly. "It's not just unintelligible noise, it talks to me. It threatened me! ...and who in the world still has a fax machine?"

The detective raised an eyebrow and looked at me quizzically.

"Look, I'm sorry but- I know what I heard and I know that whatever this is, it's intentional. Is there anything you can do?"

The detective grabbed a notebook and began writing something down, he spoke without looking up from his paper.

"We'll open an investigation. Unfortunately, with these types of things, it becomes quite difficult without a proper phone number to track down. I can't guarantee anything but I would suggest either recording your next call so we have some harder evidence, otherwise... maybe just change your phone number?"

He flipped the page in his notebook and continued to fill out some sort of form.

"B-but... I can't just change my number, I need my phone for my work, for my family... my mother is too old to remember something new. I can't-"

"Sir, with all due respect, we have very pressing matters to deal with on a daily basis here. Until your crank caller becomes a legitimate threat, it's not exactly going to jump to the top of our list."

Crank caller!? I was furious but what was the point? I had nothing left to give them, they had nothing else that could help me. I went home and tried to go about my day without hearing the echoes of metallic screams in my head.

The next few nights I slept with my phone off again. Or tried at least, I was able to sleep here and there but I was tossing and turning all throughout. And of course, every night at 3:33am I would wake up like clockwork. No phone. No calls. Still, I was on edge every time until I fell back asleep. And of course, every morning, when I turned my phone back on, there would be a new message left by a new strange number and I would be too afraid to listen. And I can't explain why but each time it feels like whatever it is, it's getting closer, like it's coming for me. I've been so out of sorts from all of this that I've had to call in sick at my job and work from home.

******

So that's where I'm at now. Sitting at the desk in my home office, trying to get some work done but instead I'm typing this story because honestly, I don't know what's going to happen to me. At least this way I'll have a record of my story in case something does happen. I took the battery out of my phone. I should call my mom but, I can't even look at that thingggggggggggg,;

***** *⁄*⁄*

3:34am…

Oh no. No no no! I fell asleep at the desk and was ripped out my sleep one minute ago by earth shaking vibrations running throughout my house. The walls, my desk, my head were all buzzing and ringing. That ringing, I didn't understand where it was coming from at first. That ringing wouldn't stop. I whirled around when I realized what it was. The ancient fax machine I have in my office, (of course I'm the only one in the world that still has one) one of those old grey ones with the big green button and the phone with a cord that's impossible to untangle. It's been ringing now for a solid minute and it feels like a grandfather clock chiming in my skull. Another strange string of numbers and letters is showing on the caller id; 52454e444552204953205245414c

I'm trying to finish writing this but the ringing won't stop and this unsettling image keeps flashing on the screen of my computer. It's hard to make out because it looks so glitchy and fractured, but it looks like a man in a suit with black leather gloves, standing in an empty board room. He's very tall and lanky but his stance is imposing. He has a perfectly sculpted hairline but his toothy smile is too long and his eye sockets are torn out. It only shows for a second before disappearing but every time it does my PC freezes up and lets out this eerie, electronic death rattle. Between this and the ringing I can hardly focus. It's like five thousand vibrating needles stabbing into my brain over and over.

I'm very scared.

I have to end this.

I'm picking it up now.

If anything happens to me,
Tell my mother

I love her 01101001 00100111 01101101
00100000 01110011 01101111 01110010
01110010 01111001

00 WE'RE SORRY

THIS STORY CAN NOT BE COMPLETED AS
DIALED.

PLEASE CLOSE THE BOOK,
AND TRY AGAIN.

ERROR MESSAGE:
01000101 0100111001000100

The Shadow Machines

"Veni Umbra Machina"

On an early Saturday afternoon in the foyer of her humble modular home, Mrs. Luckton was shushing and consoling her 4-year-old daughter, trying desperately to calm her down. Mrs. Luckton's daughter Isabel had been playing outside only a half hour earlier when one of the neighborhood bullies had walked by with his friend. Isabel was playing with her favorite pink, glittery bouncing ball and when it accidentally rolled into the street. Isabel thought the boys would lend a hand and throw it back but instead, the bully grabbed her ball and ran away laughing maniacally with lackey in tow. Isabel had screamed after them to give it back but it was no use, the boys were halfway down the block before she even made it down the driveway, she ran back into her home and started screaming and crying and stomping.

"Sweety, sweety, listen to me," said her mother as she got down to her level and grabbed her shoulders gently, "Daddy will find this mean little boy and he will have a *very* stern talk with him and he *will* get your ball back I promise."

It was not enough; Isabel didn't believe her because she knew her father. She knew he would be too tired to be bothered and even if he did, that mean boy has probably already popped her ball or lost it, or worse. She pulled away from her mother's arms and stomped and wailed some more.

"Okay, okay sweetie well… we can get you another ball! That thing was what? 3 credits? We'll get you a brand new one that's even shinier than the last one! We can go today!"

"I DON'T WANT A NEW ONE! I WANT *MY* BALL! IT'S NOT THE SAME!" she screamed in her mother's face. Isabel was so mad at her mother for not understanding she wanted to hit her.

"Well I don't appreciate your attitude young lady!" her mother snapped back, "I am trying everything I can here! You are not being fair to Mommy."

"I don't *want* Mommy!" Isabel shot back. She didn't mean it, but Isabel tended to shout the most hurtful things she could think of when she was upset.

Mrs. Luckton let out a small gasp and then crossed her arms, "well I don't want your bad attitude," she said sternly, "and maybe when the Shadow Machines come looking for naughty children, maybe I'll just let them take you away!"

With that, Isabel's mother stormed off to her own room and slammed the door. Isabel's eyes welled up with tears, surely, she thought, Mommy couldn't be serious... Her parents would never let the NaughtyBots take her or her siblings away... would they? That would be terribly mean of them to just let some big scary robots take away their loving children. Isabel was terrified but she was also angry at the thought. So angry she couldn't help but have another outburst.

"NO THANK YOU MOMMY!" she screamed as she picked up a stuffed rabbit and threw it at her mother's bedroom door as hard as she could. She thought for sure that would get a reaction out of her, she knew it would not be a good reaction but really, she just wanted her to come back out into the living room, regardless of how mad she would be. Isabel did not like being alone. She stared at the shut door with tears in her eyes and waited for it to fling open but, nothing. The room was silent, other than Isabel's heavy breathing and Mommy's door was not moving. She stood there for another minute in silence until suddenly, she heard a noise coming from outside.

Whirrrr-zhirrr-whirrr-zhirrrr-whirrr-zhirrrr

"Oh no, oh no oh no" she said to herself, It couldn't be them, could it? She thought. She listened again and heard the noise once more, still coming from outside but this time getting even louder.

Whirrrr-zhirrr-clatank-clatank-whirrr-zhirrrr-clatank-clatank!

Now she was sure it was a Shadow Machine. She could hear the metal hooves clanking against the pavement and the whirring of the gears and motors inside of the robot, it must have been only a few houses away. Isabel stood frozen in place and let out a whimpering call for her mother.

"Mommy..." her voice was quiet and shaky. Mrs. Luckton had not heard Isabel's call.

Isabel turned her head slowly to look out the bay window of their family room. Sure enough, rounding the corner of their home was a clanking, clamoring shadow machine. The machine stood about 4 feet tall, it looked like a metallic mini horse with no neck or head and inverted spindly legs, its torso was flat and covered in gears and gaskets and leather straps with flat black pads on its back for strapping in and carrying away naughty children. It also had a drooping cargo net hanging from it's under carriage to take away the smaller ones. On the very front of its torso was a round black dome that encased one camera, one speaker, one scanner and one spotlight, all spread out to look like bug eyes on the rotating mound. When the machine got to the front of Isabel's house it slowed down its trot to a creeping prancing motion, when it got to her door it stopped completely and played a very eerie recorded message. It was a computerized woman's voice.

"Do I hear any naughty naughty children? Does someone need to be taken away to learn more about happiness and kindness?" the voice was made to sound light and airy, to make you feel calm but it only came off as unnerving and creepy... it sent chills through each one of Isabel's bones. The message began to repeat as the thing crept closer to their door, "Do I hear any naughty naughty chil-"

"Mommy!" cried Isabel, desperate to be held in her mother's loving arms but still too petrified to move from where she was.

"Isabel?" the bedroom door flew open and Mrs. Luckton sprinted across the hall to her child. "Oh no! Oh baby I didn't really mean it! I-I didn't think they would actually come!"

"Mommy I'm scared!" Isabel sobbed uncontrollably into her mother's side.

They heard the robot once again from the other side of their front door, "Naughty child detected. Entering domicile for extraction. Your consent and/or cooperation is not needed, we will take your child for corrections." the machine's voice sounded more aggressive with every word. It began to unlock the door with a lockpicking mechanism that had sprang out of its torso, but just as the door began to open the machine was stopped by another noise outside.

"Hey look Tevin, it's one of those stupid wussy NaughtyBots!" it was the bullies from earlier that day, marching back down the street like they owned it, "My dad used to work on them, he said they have a weak spot riiight behind the left-*leg!*" said the boy as he laughed and kicked the robots back leg in an attempt to take it out. The Shadow Machine stumbled and lost its footing for a second, it stumbled off the Luckton's front steps but regained its balance before falling to the floor. The robot whirled around quickly and scanned the two boys. Its digitized voice rang out, "Target acquired! Commencing extraction!"

Long metal wires shot out and wrapped around the first boy. His friend Tevin shrieked and sprinted away as fast as he could. For Isabel's bully however, it was too late for an escape, the shadow machine pulled him onto it's back and quickly strapped him down so he could not squirm away and started to trot back down the street. The Luckton's slammed the door closed, locked it and held each other tighter than they ever had.

"Mommy?" Isabel looked up at her mother, still shaking and sobbing quietly.

"Yes sweety?"

"I'm sorry, I'm so sorry and I swear-" her mother cut her off and squeezed Isabel against her chest.

"No sweetheart, *I'm* sorry, and I promise I will *never* let you go."

They rocked back and forth in a tight embrace and listened to the screams of a naughty child being carried off into the distance.

The Red Square in the White Room

When Micah awoke, he was not sure exactly how long he had been sleeping. Nor was he sure of where he was or how he arrived there. Micah's head felt murky and everything seemed to be bathed in a bright white fog, it took his eyes a few minutes before they could focus on anything. When he was finally coherent enough to take in his surroundings, he felt a sudden wave of panic run through his body. He looked frantically in every direction to confirm if his fears were true and indeed, they were. Micah was now aware that he was somehow trapped inside of a white room no bigger than his own bedroom with white walls a white floor and white ceiling. As far as he could see, there were no doors or windows. Unsure how the room was even being illuminated, Micah looked for a light fixture but all he could see was solid white walls surrounding him. Micah shuffled his feet as he looked around and flinched when he abruptly felt something soft and fleshy beneath him. He jumped back and looked at where he had been standing. There in the center of the floor was one shiny red tile. Micah got down on his hands and knees to examine the red square even closer. Once he got closer, he noticed that it wasn't a tile at all, it looked like something organic. What it looked like was skin, or an open wound, like someone had peeled off one square of white tile in the floor and beneath it was another square of oozing bloody flesh. He stared at the red square for quite some time before getting up and walking backwards to one of the corners of the room. He wanted to touch the red but he was afraid of it, something about it was unsettling, the red seemed to serve as a warning. At the same time, something was telling Micah that the red square was the key to figuring out what this white room was and how to get out of it. He turned and ran his fingers along the wall, it was cold to the touch and hard as bone. It looked like drywall but felt like concrete, Micah knocked on it once searching for a hollow spot but it was rock solid. He walked along the perimeter wrapping his knuckles up and down the walls but there was no give, might as well have been a white stone tomb. Micah stopped and put his back against one of the walls, he needed to regroup and gather his thoughts. Micah tried to think of the last thing he remembered before waking up in this alabaster prison. His memory was clouded and defragmented, every image he tried to conjure was blurred or scratched out. He seemed to remember trying or wanting to go to sleep but even that notion felt like a false memory. What was this place? Why was everything so stark? He rubbed his eyes and pushed off of the wall. Micah looked up towards the flat cream-colored roof above, he couldn't quite tell how far away it was from him. He tried to jump and touch it but couldn't reach. It almost felt like it moved away from his hand as he jumped. Was this room moving around him? It was hard to see what was stationary and what was static, the only definition in the room was the slightly gray shadowed lines of each corner and the squared rouge blemish in the center of the floor. Micah started to walk again stretching out his arms until they touched the ghostly walls on his side, he quickly got to one corner of the room but as he walked to the next it seemed to take forever. He began to feel more and more claustrophobic with every step. Had the room gotten longer? He walked to the middle of the room towards the red square and looked around at the walls, now it felt smaller. When he looked up at the ceiling again, it felt like it was coming down on him. Micah's breathing became short and rapid, his vision blurred, he felt sick, dizzy. Micah dropped to his knees and grabbed onto the floor, it was just as smooth as the walls, Micah wanted to throw up but he felt nothing in his stomach. After a few deep breaths Micah started to calm down, he closed his eyes and immediately regretted it. Perhaps because his eyes had been bathing in an ocean of milky white walls or perhaps because he was feeling so nauseous it was all his mind could process, but when Micah closed his eyes all he saw was more white. Blank, bright, blinding white. It was like he blinked and got transported into the same room again. Micah clutched his stomach and fell on his side staring up at the room. He wanted to cry but no tears came to his eyes, they were dry and burning. He moved his head and looked at the red square on the floor, at this point it was the only thing that wasn't driving him mad. He crawled over to the glossy red patch. Micah hovered a single finger over it as he contemplated. What kind of torture was this? Was someone playing a sick joke on him?

If this was one of those old escape room games, he wasn't having any fun. What other options do I have? He thought to himself as he pushed his index finger into the mushy red substance. As soon as he touched it, he flinched, it was as if he had plucked a violin string inside his skeleton. He pulled his hand away again. He rolled his eyes around the white room and decided that nothing could be worse than another minute in this empty void. Micah plunged his finger into the crimson mass. Electricity shot through his bones, and the further he dug his finger the more it felt like his skin was being peeled off by the sheer force of vibration. Micah pulled his hand out and gasped for air, his ears were ringing. He looked at his hand, covered in sticky blood and white puss. He looked back at the red square and noticed the hole he had started to make. He got up on hand and knee and hovered over it, he squinted at the ruby red gash for a moment. There was something coming through. If he squinted hard enough, Micah could just make out a tiny speck of light coming through the hole. Maybe this really was the key to get out, but even if it was, the square was only about the size of both his hands held together, it was far too tiny for him to squeeze through. Micah sighed and wiped his bloody hand on the floor. He looked at his red handprint for a long time, it was nice to have something other than white walls and bloody red squares to look at for once. He wiped his hand some more and left a large red streak, he laughed to himself at how pleasing it was. Micah was always squeamish, that type of thing would normally make him feel faint but looking at it now, it was like a beautiful painting. He picked up his hand to make more of a mess but when he looked at it, he noticed it was suddenly completely clean again. How? He screamed inside his head. He looked back at the smears he had left on the ground and they were also gone, replaced with more shining, immaculate white flooring. Micah spun around trying to find a trace of any red besides the square in the center of the floor but there was none. This must be a dream, he told himself. These kinds of things don't just happen, he thought. He brought his fingers up to the side of his head and pinched the side of his temple until he thought it was going to break skin. Nothing. He was wide awake in this ivory hell. He looked back at the red square, the hole he had begun to dig was still there. That was it, there was no other escape. Maybe at the very least he could get through and see what was on the other side, maybe even scream for help. He crouched down over the red shape and plunged his fist into the gaping wound. The pain was like a burning meteorite had crashed through his own skull. Every time he moved his arm, he felt his whole body shake like a human tuning fork. Micah pushed through the pain, he grit his teeth so hard he thought they would shatter in his mouth. He pushed harder. Finally, he felt something break through. He felt cold frigid air on the other side. Salvation! He plunged his other hand into the square and dug like a mad man, every inch of the way felt as if his own skeleton was trying to rip its way out of his skin but Micah didn't care. Escape was the only thing he could think of. He pushed and clawed and dug until the square was wide open and pouring through the other side was an iridescent light. "Great, more white light," he joked to himself, but this light was different. There was a shimmering rainbow-colored glow along the edges, and something about it was warm and inviting. Micah knew that this was the way out but he was scared to leave. What if it was just another white room on the other side? It was a chance he'd have to take. Micah took one last, deep gulp of air and put his face into the square.   A cool breeze brushed against his forehead, it was   welcoming him in. The closer he got he felt the square grow wider and wider, or maybe his body was getting smaller and smaller, he couldn't tell. Micah slid into the widening vortex and escaped from the limbo he was trapped in. Micah suddenly recognized his surroundings. He was in his own room only, he felt taller. He was definitely higher than he should have been, his head was almost touching the ceiling. He also felt lighter and airier than he had before. Micah looked down and felt dizzy again, he was floating, and directly beneath him was his own body lying lifeless in his own bed. "How?" He tried to say out loud but no words came out. Before he could ask anything else Micah was ripped away from himself, far away from his bed and his body and far, far away from that terrible white room,

into

the

e t h e r.

Backword

For the record; Every one of these stories was created and collected by me, C.J. Sampera. If a strange shapeshifting, anthropomorphic, crazy and *cranky* old crow person going by the name Lord Noctulis tries to tell you that they compiled and transcribed these stories themselves, please do your best to ignore them. They are absolutely insane and in no place to claim that *I* stole these stories when *they* know good and well what *they* have stolen, and how much chaos *they* have unleashed on the world as a result. That old bird should be so lucky... any ways, I hope you enjoyed and endured! Each legend carries its own weight, don't let it stick with you too long...
Until the next volume,

-C.J.

The
Grimmsomniac's
Gallery

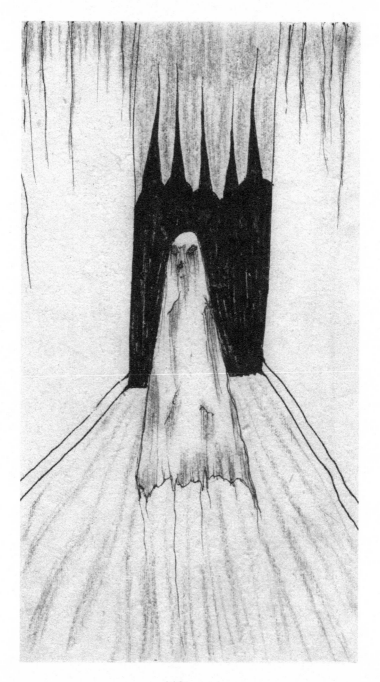

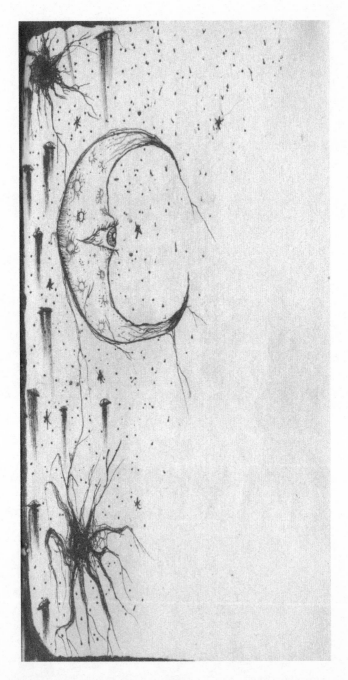

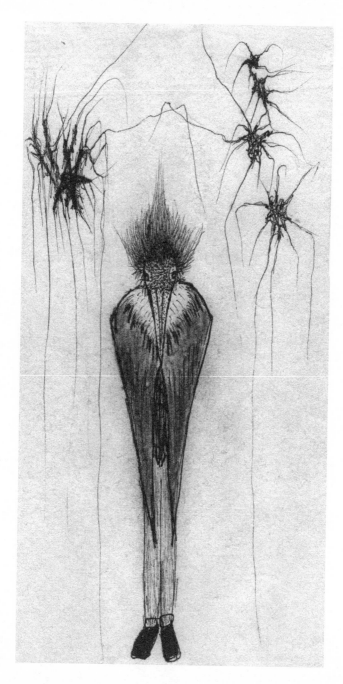

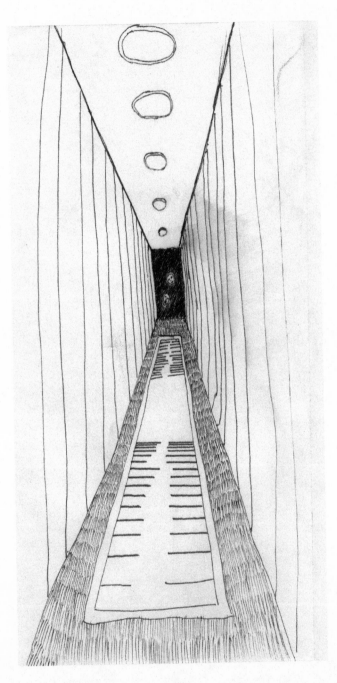

116

Lord Noctulis

Chaos Incarnate

"I watch their dreams.
I collect their nightmares."

Dominus Noct.

Unsettling Legends

Made in the USA
Las Vegas, NV
22 August 2021